FIGHTING

EL FUEGO

BY

PETE BIRLE

el fuego is Spanish for "the fire."

Scobre Press Corporation
2255 Calle Clara
La Jolla, CA 92037

Scobre Press books may be purchased for
educational, business or sales promotional use.

Edited by Helen Glenn Court
Illustrated by Gail Piazza
Cover Design by Michael Lynch

ISBN 1-933423-28-5

HOME RUN EDITION

www.scobre.com

CHAPTER ONE

EL FUEGO

"How's that feel?" A lean black man in his sixties wraps another layer of tape around my right hand. I make a fist and slam it into the open palm of my left. The thwack it makes lets me know that the taping job is first-rate.

"Feels good," I answer, sliding off the training table and standing upright. I begin throwing punches at an imaginary opponent. Shadowboxing, as it's called, is the best way to warm up before a fight. I throw several hard jabs into the air. My nerves calm every time my arm extends.

"Stand still," the man says firmly. I stop in my tracks. He begins to put a thin coat of Vaseline on my face. I hate the slippery feel of the Vaseline. Still, I know how important it is. I try not to move while he rubs it in. In a few minutes, I'll be glad it's there.

When my opponent hits my face, his glove will slide. "This goo is gonna help you from ending up with a face like mine," the old man laughs.

I force a smile. I wonder if my face will ever look like his. "Thanks," I say softly.

He nods his head in a knowing way. He then winks at me and says, "Don't worry, kid. You ain't gonna end up as ugly as me." I smile again, for real this time.

Throughout this process, a serious-faced official watches over us. I throw a few more punches into the air, finishing with an uppercut. I think about my parents, my coach and my brother. Suddenly my heart is racing. I realize in this moment how desperately I want to win tonight. Not just for me, but for all of them.

Once finished, the old man puts down his roll of tape and jar of grease. He picks up a pair of gloves and shoves them onto my hands. He laces them up, tight, and he slaps them hard with his hands. The room is now quiet. I begin hopping around again, throwing more punches into the air. My hands are adjusting to the gloves. After a few minutes, I can't even feel the gloves—they have become a part of my hands. I am now completely focused, ready to fight.

"Stay still," the old man repeats. "We're not finished." I stop moving again as he helps me into my headgear. The padded helmet amateur boxers wear for protection fits snugly on my head. He steps out of the way so the official can approve his work. As the old man turns to leave, he shouts over his shoulder. *"Buena suerte."* Good luck to you. I nod.

I watch as the former boxer-turned-trainer makes his way toward the exit. The room is once again completely quiet. That's exactly the way I like it before a bout. But the old man still has to open the door to get out. When he does, all the noise from the crowded arena pours in on me. It's loud out there. Although the cheering gets my adrenaline pumping, I look forward to the silence returning.

The door clicks closed and I am alone with the official. He opens a folding chair and sits in the far corner of the locker room. I start to throw a few more punches into the air, practicing a powerful combination. I know that this fight will take all of my strength. It will also take every ounce of my self-control. For a boxer to be successful, he needs to control his emotions. He needs to stick to his game plan. Fighting on emotion does not work in the ring. I learned this lesson as a kid—the hard way.

My breathing is a little heavier now. I've done a decent job warming up. I can hear my heart beating and nothing else.

I'm eighteen years old and getting ready to fight in the Olympic Box-offs. I'm here at the Olympic Training Center in Colorado, home of the U.S. team. Just being here is a dream come true. But I'm not going to stop now. I want to make the team, rep-

resent my country, and bring home gold. In a few minutes, I am going to be fighting the most important fight of my life. It will determine my fate as an Olympic boxer. If I win, I go to the Summer Games in San José, Costa Rica. If I lose, I go home.

I'm in the best shape of my life. At five feet, seven inches tall, I now weigh a solid 140 pounds. I'm ready to become America's representative in the light welterweight division. My opponent is the nephew of a former world champion. His uncle held the professional junior middleweight title for several years. Most of the newspapers are predicting his victory over me. I don't care. I know what I have to do to win, and I plan to do it.

I walk past the silent official and over to a mirror hanging on the wall. I take a long look at myself. First, I glance down at my white shorts with the blue beltline. Then, I stare at my white tank top and red sneakers. I proudly wear the colors of the American flag. Yet, I know these colors also represent Puerto Rico—the country where my parents were born. These colors remind me of my responsibility to my family. And to the two places I love.

For me, life wasn't always this exciting. I hadn't always felt a love of country, or even a love of myself. There was a time when I never could have imagined representing anything. Back in the day, I didn't pursue any goals and I didn't have any dreams. I didn't even know who I was. I was lost. If you knew me when I was a kid, you never would have believed I could come this far.

Standing in front of the mirror, I stare into my dark brown eyes. I look past the pupils, deep into my heart. "There you are," I whisper. "El Fuego." I can still see it in my eyes—the fire, the beast. Sure, I've learned to control it over the years by long ago burying it somewhere deep inside of myself. But I know that fire is still dangerous. And I know that I will always have to keep an eye on it. Because once ignited, el fuego will burn out of control. And it will take me down with it.

When I was a kid, anger ran my life. I never knew when an explosion was coming. Once it started—and el fuego took hold—I couldn't do anything to stop it. It was like a living thing. It breathed. It ate. It hated. And it nearly ruined my life. It was a long time before I realized I couldn't kill this fire raging inside. It was part of me. I had to live with it. I had to learn to control it.

In the middle of these thoughts, the locker room door opens again. I turn away from the mirror as the noise from the crowd rushes in. This time the door stays open. I put my robe on and throw a few jabs into the air. I stare out toward the lights of the arena. Now my heart is really racing. Smack! I hit my gloves together and turn toward the door.

The old man speaks to me again. "Let's go, kid, fight night."

CHAPTER TWO

RECESS

My name is Francisco Diaz. Only, I didn't like being called Francisco when I was twelve. I didn't like being called Francis, Frankie, or Frank, either. I went by my nickname, Paco. And when I told someone to call me Paco, I meant it.

Although I was born in Philadelphia, my folks came from the island of Puerto Rico. They moved to Philly right after they got married. When they decided to start a family, they moved down to Rock River. Across the Delaware River from New Jersey, Rock River has been our home ever since.

Like many American-born Hispanics, I'm bilingual. When I was little, my parents always spoke Spanish at home. Even though we lived in Pennsylvania, Spanish was my first language. By the time I got to kindergarten, though, I spoke perfect English. Dad said

I learned by watching television. I didn't think it was quite that simple. I remember hundreds of conversations I had with my older brother in English. Speaking with him helped me learn the language as well. It was just like Dad to forget details that involved my brother.

I looked like your average sixth-grader. I was short and skinny, with black hair and strong Latin features. Although I may have looked like the other kids at St. Joe's Elementary School, I didn't act like them. I remember one incident on the playground that really singled me out as a problem child. It also ended up changing my life.

His name was Butchie LaManna, and he thought he was hot stuff. He was two grades ahead of me. Butchie was the typical eighth-grade bully. He picked on smaller and weaker sixth-graders. He'd approach the younger kids on the playground. Then he'd scare them into giving up their basketball or handing over their baseball cards. He did that kind of thing pretty much every day.

Of course, Butchie always had his two buddies, Tommy and Ray Ray, with him. I looked at Butchie and his crew as an annoyance. I could avoid them easily. After all, I kept pretty much to myself back then.

One afternoon in early October, Butchie made a mistake. He'd obviously heard about my reputation as a troublemaker, someone you didn't mess with.

This reputation had followed me to St. Joe's from the last school I was kicked out of. It also made me a target for Butchie. In his mind, taking me down would make him the toughest kid in school.

I was minding my own business that day, leaning against the fence. Standing alone at recess was not uncommon for me. I would always watch the rest of the kids talking and playing ball. Usually, I'd be looking at a comic book.

I was a loner. This wasn't because I wanted to be one. I just was. I'm not really sure why. I do know that I was good at pushing people away—literally. I saw my fair share of the principal's office back then. I was constantly getting into fights. In short, I was a mixed-up, high-strung, angry kid. Or at least that's what everyone told me. So I just went with it.

I didn't know how messed up I was until Butchie approached me that day.

"Hey, Diaz!" Butchie called out. He walked toward me with his two stooges following close behind.

I tried to ignore him, but he wouldn't quit. "I'm talking to you, Pah-coh!" he said. He was louder this time as he made fun of my Hispanic accent.

Just about everyone on the playground heard him. Just about everyone stopped what they were doing to watch. Even the girls practicing their double-dutch jump-roping stopped—and those girls never stopped.

Butchie had addressed me by my last name and then again by my nickname. It would have been rude not to respond. As if I cared. I had already made a career out of being rude. I said nothing. I wasn't interested in a conversation. And I didn't care what the consequences were.

"Are you deaf or something?" asked Butchie. "Or are you just stupid?"

I remember looking up at him blankly. I stared into his eyes, the anger building up inside me. At that point, I couldn't think about anything besides slamming my fist into Butchie's face. My right hand started to curl into a tight ball. My left hand followed a moment later. If he could have read my mind, he would have stopped messing with me. But he didn't.

The funny thing was that I wasn't a big kid. In fact, I was kind of scrawny back then. My small frame and unkempt black hair made me look like a geek, too. Yet, even at twelve years old, I was strong. I was a volcano of energy. When I was mad, I would erupt. And as Butchie got closer, things were really starting to rumble inside of me.

"I'm talking to you, Diaz," he continued. The bully was now inches away from me. He and his friends were determined to see this thing through. "You have something I want."

I knew he was talking about the comic book I was holding. But I wasn't going to say anything. I was so blinded by rage that I couldn't speak even if I had wanted to. All I could do was glare at Butchie. I could feel my heart rate quicken. The rumble inside of me was getting louder and louder. The sound was like an approaching train—and Butchie was standing on the tracks. It was getting hard to ignore.

"Everybody's right, you are a wacko." Butchie shook his head from side to side as he spoke. "I just wanted to see your comic book for a minute, Diaz. Now it looks like I'm going to have to take it from you." He looked over at Tommy and Ray Ray. "Don't worry. He's not so tough. Are you, Pah-coh?" As he spoke, he reached out and grabbed the comic from my hand.

As he did, I decided to respond. I didn't say a word, though. The rumble inside of me exploded— the train had arrived. And there was nothing I could do to stop it.

I remember the first punch I hit Butchie with. It was a hard right hand to his cheek. I turned to Tommy and Ray Ray, who were already running across the playground. I wanted to give them a dose of the same medicine. But they wouldn't have any of it. After my punch connected, I decided it was time to say something. "Looks like you're on your own, Butchie."

Raising his hands, he started to circle around me. It was clear he wasn't afraid to fight. "You should have given up your comic book, Diaz," Butchie said. "Because now you're in big trouble."

Many principals had given my parents the same

report on me for years now: I lashed out. I attacked others, many of whom didn't fight back. I fought dirty. I punched first. I never apologized. I was a monster.

In this case, though, my enemy was willing to fight back. Unfortunately, that only fueled my fire. I was already a servant to my master—el fuego. I had neither the desire nor the ability to change my plans. I was caught in el fuego's clutches. It was destiny. I would fight.

I remember the two of us pounding each other. Butchie hit me with his fists. I hit him with my hands, my elbows, my forehead, my knees, and my feet. When he'd hit me, I'd strike back like a madman. Although Butchie was much bigger than me, I was landing the majority of the blows. I can't remember the specifics, though. Things would get fuzzy for me when I was in the middle of a fight. The rage and the fury would take over, and I would operate on impulse. On blind instinct. Like a cornered animal. It was scary. The truth was that I had no control over myself. And during this time in my life, I really hated myself. I think deep down, I wanted to get better. I just didn't know how.

As the fight unfolded, many of the kids on the playground looked scared or upset. Some turned their heads. Even those who moved closer had strange expressions on their faces. They looked disturbed by what they were witnessing. It was the playground version of a carnival, and I was the disgusting freak.

I remember Butchie popping me in the face with

his left. I tried to grab him, hoping to wrestle him to the ground. But I couldn't force his big body to the pavement. Every time I got a hold of him, he'd hit me in the torso. I felt pain around my eye and along my chest. Instead of respecting the source of that pain, I ignored it. I let el fuego overrule common sense. It was my rage that helped me to finally knock Butchie down. And it took a sneaky kick to the groin to do it. Once he was doubled over on the blacktop, I didn't back off. Although part of me knew I shouldn't, the rest of me couldn't stop.

Mr. Bermudez was the fifth-grade teacher on duty at recess that day. He finally made it over to stop the fight. Sixty-one years old, he was dressed in a brown suit and tie. He had to run all the way across the playground to reach us.

Now, this next part I don't remember at all. I was told about it later in the principal's office. When Mr. Bermudez arrived, I was apparently standing over Butchie LaManna and was just about to jump on him. El fuego was burning, and I was obviously still crazed. Seeing this, Mr. Bermudez reached out to pull me away. That's when I turned toward St. Joe's oldest and most respected teacher—and bit him on the arm.

CHAPTER THREE

A BAD SEED

As principal of St. Joe's, Mrs. Grace had a file on every student. It didn't take her long to find mine. It did take her a while to pull it out of her desk, though. It was pretty thick. St. Joe's was my third school in three years. My parents had hoped the discipline and special attention it provided would address my problems.

I poked at my new black eye with my finger. I looked at Mrs. Grace. Then, I looked at my folks. I guessed St. Joe's wasn't the answer.

"Francisco," she began.

I immediately interrupted her. "My name is Paco," I said.

My mother sighed. My father shot me a look of disapproval.

Mrs. Grace seemed to ignore my comment. I

looked across the desk at her. I know I should have respected her as principal of the school, but I didn't. She looked up at me, her eyes missing the warmth they usually showed. "This is the final straw, Francisco," she said. "The way you acted today was simply disgraceful." For the first time since I met her, Mrs. Grace sounded mean.

I looked down at my shoes. There was still some of Butchie's blood on them.

She continued talking. "This was the fourth fight you've been in since joining us six weeks ago. Even worse, this is also the second teacher you've assaulted. I'm not even going to discuss the disrespect you've displayed in the classroom. You have all the makings of a bad seed, young man," she added. Her voice took on an even sharper tone.

I knew what was coming. My dad had said it when he and Mom enrolled me at St. Joe's. One more visit with the principal and my next stop would be military school. "Your father has mentioned a military school to me. Under the circumstances, I don't think it's a bad idea." Mrs. Grace leaned forward. "However, you might end up getting kicked out of there as well. And then, where would we turn?" She sighed deeply. "So, until we learn what's making you behave this way, we'll keep you here. Even if it has to be under lock and key." Turning to my parents, she continued. "I think we should see what we're dealing with here before anyone does something drastic. That's why," she turned back to me, "I'm recommending you see a psychologist."

My older brother JoJo and I did everything together. We walked to school together. We rode bikes together. We went to the movies together. We shared the same room, the same clothes, and the same fears and dreams. We were best friends.

José Diaz, my brother's real name, was my hero. To me, JoJo was the greatest guy in the world. He found time to hang out with me, teach me things, and tell me jokes. I always wanted to be around him, and he didn't mind me tagging along most of the time. I think he even enjoyed it. I wanted to grow up to be just like him.

Then, one day, he was gone. Out of my life forever. Just like that. Two policemen knocked on the door to our apartment one night during dinner. They grabbed my brother, shoving him into the back seat of their car. I stood there crying as they drove away with him. He was fifteen. I was eight.

It turns out that JoJo had joined a local gang. To become a member, he had committed a crime. A serious crime. A violent crime. Because of it he was sent away to prison for a long time.

My parents disowned him. At my father's command, his name was never to be spoken in our apartment again. Whatever pictures there were of JoJo were either thrown away or put in the closet. My baby sister Marisol was only three when JoJo left. By the time she turned five, she hardly remembered him.

But I did. I remembered him. I thought about him every day. From the night he was taken away, to the morning he went off to prison. And every day since.

Before JoJo was locked up, I was your typical second-grader. Even when all of this trouble unfolded with my brother, I didn't freak out. Not right away at least. Except for becoming quieter, I dealt with my brother being a criminal pretty well. For a while, that is.

A year later, by the time I was nine, things changed. I started to feel really angry about what happened to JoJo. I was angry at the police for taking him away. I was angry at the gang for wanting him. I was angry at him for leaving me. I was angry at my parents for disowning him. I felt like nothing in my life mattered. So I stopped caring about doing the right thing. I stopped being polite. I stopped smiling and laughing. I stopped making friends, hugging my mother, respecting my father, doing well in school. None of it mattered to me.

I was on my own. To protect myself from getting hurt again, I stopped caring about anything or anyone—including myself.

CHAPTER FOUR

KILLER INSTINCT

So this was it, I remember thinking, as I exited my parents' car. My next stop wasn't going to be the Army. It was here, at a shrink's office.

Dr. Adriana Colòn was a former St. Joe's student. She completed high school in three years, went on to college, and then medical school. She had always been a favorite of Principal Grace's. That's because she came home to Rock River to practice child psychology. Smart and attractive, Dr. Colòn was the pride of Rock River's Puerto Rican community. I seemed to be the curse.

She was waiting for us at the top of the stairs. As I approached her, I thought about what my dad had said moments earlier "If this doesn't work, you'll be wearing a Hill Valley Military School uniform." I had to admit that the thought of attending military school scared me.

Like I said, deep down, I wanted to change. And not just because I was scared of being sent away. Being out of control was a scary thing in itself. Life was no fun for me. I had nobody and nothing. Still, I didn't think there wasn't anything I could do to tame el fuego.

Dr. Colòn invited us into the waiting room that led to her office. "Good afternoon," she said, extending her hand for me to shake. "You must be Paco." I was surprised and satisfied that she called me by the name I preferred. Still, I avoided eye contact when I shook her hand.

"Hola Señor y Señora Diaz," she said to my folks in Spanish. "You two can wait here while Paco and I talk in my office."

All of a sudden, I didn't feel too well. Just being in a psychologist's office was making me sick. I knew this lady was going to ask me a lot of questions about my feelings. I really hated talking about my feelings.

Following Dr. Colòn inside her office, I glanced back at my folks. I know my face showed how I felt, and that wasn't good. My mom gave me a look of encouragement. My dad just glared at me. I immediately looked at the floor. I was ashamed.

I knew Dad was disappointed in me—really disappointed. My father, a roofer and part-time builder, was a man's man. He was wiry with long arms. But his body was hard just like his will. He never let his emotions get the best of him. He thought a man's ability to not blow his cool was his greatest strength. He also thought people who acted out physically when pushed were weak. This was why he reacted so harshly to JoJo's arrest. And why the thought of me having to see a therapist was so upsetting. To him, my brother and I possessed something he didn't—some weakness, some defect. It led us to act out.

I was really starting to think my father disliked me. Like everything else in my life, this made me angry. He, much more than my mom, was at the end of his rope. I heard him tell my mother that exact thing two nights earlier. At this time in my life, my father and I had a pretty bad relationship. I believe now that my father did want to see me get better. He desperately wanted to fix in me what he couldn't fix in JoJo. I know he loved me. He just didn't know how to show it back then.

Of course, my mother was my on my side— she always had been. She continued to encourage me no matter how I behaved. I didn't find out until later, but she never wanted to take down JoJo's pictures or disown him. My brother and I had crushed our mom's spirit with our bad choices. She was sad all the time. Her two sons had been the light of her life just a few years earlier. Now, with JoJo gone and me acting out, all she knew was grief and despair.

In my heart, I knew how badly Mom wanted

her smiling, happy son back. I felt guilty every time I looked at her. Yet, it was impossible for me to show love toward her. I had convinced myself that the loving boy she was looking for was gone.

My parents had a lot of arguments. All of them were about their different approaches to what they called my issues. More and more, I was the topic of conversation at the dinner table. I was the subject of the shouting I heard coming from their bedroom. "You don't want him to end up like the other one, do you?" Dad would say.

They had been in enough principals' offices—and they were tired of it. They were hoping this psychologist could make some sense out of me.

"So, Paco," Dr. Colòn asked, sitting down in a big armchair. "How are you today?"

I had sat down on the couch opposite her. The office reminded me of a living room, not a doctor's office. But I still didn't feel at home. I fidgeted in my seat. I was uncomfortable, and I'm sure it showed. "Good," I answered, looking away. I glanced out the window over Dr. Colòn's shoulder. I'd have given anything to be outside in the crisp fall air—away from this office and all my problems. I opened the top button of my shirt. It was starting to get warm in there.

"I'm glad to hear that," she said. Her voice was soothing but it didn't put me at ease. I could feel my heart beating faster. My armpits dampened with sweat.

"Well," she said, grabbing a notebook from off

the coffee table in front of her. She then pulled a pen from the inside pocket of her blazer. "We've got a lot to talk about, so why don't we get started?"

I moved around in my seat again. I hated this situation. I hated being in this warm room, talking to this stranger. "Okay," I said with a hint of anger in my voice. "So, what am I supposed to say? You're the doctor, right? Shouldn't you say something first?"

She smiled. "I'm much more interested in hearing from you. First of all, relax, Paco. This is not a test," Dr. Colòn said. "I just want to get to know you better. Why don't you start by telling me what you like to do?"

I didn't know what to say. So I just blurted out the first thing that popped into my head. "Um, I like watching baseball sometimes."

"Me, too," she responded. "I'm a big Phillies fan. I hope this is the year we finally beat the Braves. What else do you like?"

Honestly, I wasn't a big baseball fan at all. But I had to say something. Still, hearing Dr. Colòn talk about the Phillies made me a bit more comfortable. If nothing else, it took my mind off being in a psychologist's office. So I started talking more. I mentioned my comic books, television shows I liked, and video games I played. For the next twenty minutes, I talked a lot.

In the middle of talking about this stuff, I figured something out: Dr. Colòn was buttering me up—

actually, setting me up. She was just waiting to ask me about my feelings. I stopped talking as suddenly as I had started. Then I looked at her with a sly smile that said, "What do you really want to talk about?" That's when I started to lose control a little. It wasn't that I was surprised by what Dr. Colòn was trying to do. In fact, I knew what was happening from the start. Principal Grace didn't send me here to talk about comic books and video games.

My breathing started to get heavier and I leaned forward. "I'm done talking for now."

Dr. Colòn noticed my mood change. "Tell me what you're feeling right now, Paco. Tell me what you feel when you're about to lose control?"

Just then, I felt a pain in my neck. The blood was rushing to my head. I had actually been stupid enough to trust this lady. She was just like the rest of them! I was starting to get really mad. The unease I had been feeling began to fuel my fire. I could feel el fuego coming on. Yet, at that moment, I really didn't want to explode. Not there. That would just prove everyone right. I actually thought about that, which was strange for me. I took a deep breath. "I don't know how I feel," I said. I tried to give an honest answer while doing my best to contain my emotions. "I know that when I'm mad sometimes, I think about my brother. Then I kind of lose it."

"Okay," she said, supportively. "Let's explore that. You love your brother, huh?" To this question, I had no response. I simply stared at the wall. Dr. Colòn kept talking. "Paco, I can only help you if you talk to me. Tell me about him. Tell me why you're so angry."

Surprisingly, this question did not make me want to attack Dr. Colòn or punch the wall. Instead, it made me think. Why was I so angry? I slumped down into the couch and began telling her everything. Things I didn't even know about myself came out. I have to admit, it felt pretty good. After an hour of talking, mostly about JoJo, things seemed okay. El fuego disappeared for the moment, and I was no longer warm and uncomfortable.

When we walked out of the office, I was exhausted. My mom noticed it immediately and put her arms around me. My dad wasn't so observant, but he did manage a smile. "Well," he said, glancing at Dr. Colòn. "What do you think?"

"Why don't you all join me back in my office," Dr. Colòn said.

Once inside, I sat back on the couch, nearly falling asleep. My parents sat one on each side of me. Dr. Colòn returned to her chair. She took off her glasses and leaned forward. "We've only had one session," she said. "So I can't tell you exactly why Paco lashes out the way he does. I do think it may have a lot to do with JoJo." The moment she mentioned this, my father looked away. She continued, "Paco is a very angry young man. This anger takes hold of him. He feels there is nothing he can do to stop it. I believe that Paco has what's called a killer instinct."

My mother gasped. My father took a deep breath. I cringed.

"What exactly is that?" my dad asked.

"It's a condition," she said. "Paco reacts with a burst of energy that he has to release when he is angered. When he gets mad, he boils over easily. And once he starts, he can't stop." She smiled over at me. "Not yet, at least."

After my diagnosis had sunk in, my mother spoke up. "So what do we do about it?"

"Well, Paco comes in to see me twice every week. Together, we'll begin to tackle his problem," Dr. Colòn said. She looked over at me. "This is something we can fix, Paco. How's that sound?"

"Great," I answered sarcastically.

Fixing my problem was not easy. During our next five sessions, Dr. Colòn and I talked about my feelings. Then, we talked about what I thought about my feelings. And we spent quite a bit of time discussing JoJo.

Dr. Colòn tried to get me to rate my level of anger on a chart. Every time I got mad, I was to take out the chart. This was easier said than done. I was to place a check next to the level of anger I was feeling. I was to use a scale of one to 100. A ten meant I was calm. A ninety meant I was out for blood. The problem was that I never recorded a number higher than twenty. Once I hit thirty, I completely forgot the chart because, after thirty, el fuego took over.

I was supposed to write down my reaction to my own anger. Did I throw something? Did I break something? Did I yell something? Recording this stuff as it happened was supposed to help me. I'd become better at realizing my problem and controlling my response. The problem was that I just couldn't do it. I was too pumped up when I was mad. I could barely speak, much less write!

At the end of three weeks, I felt like I had been beaten up. I had gotten into two more fights at school. One was a fistfight with a classmate. The other was with the crossing guard.

Dr. Colòn was still positive, despite my lack of progress. "Paco, I'm proud of you."

"For what?" I asked, sadly. "I'm not getting better. I think I may be getting worse."

She stood up and sat next to me on the couch. "I'm proud you're trying to dig deep down to explore what makes you tick. I know you'll get better because of it." Dr. Colòn said. "Still, we're not making as much progress as I had hoped. I think we need to change our thinking a bit."

Dr. Colòn stood up and looked at me strangely. "Not every kid with a killer instinct needs what I think you do."

I was listening. I wondered what she had in store for me next.

"We need to get rid of the energy that makes you explode. The energy that makes it impossible for you write down your feelings." She paused. "Here's what I'm thinking: you should buy a punching bag."

"What?" I asked in disbelief. "A punching bag?"

"Si." She smiled. "I want you to hang it up in your apartment. And when you feel angry about something, I want you to punch it," she said. "How does that sound?"

"Honestly, it sounds pretty crazy." I laughed. "But I guess I could try it. It's better than punching someone's head in, right? What's the catch?"

"There's no catch, Paco," she said. "I'm trying to help you turn down the flame on el fuego. Place your killer instinct on the back burner. Maybe this will work. I think the chart was probably not the best idea for you."

"So, you want me to actually hit something when I'm mad?"

She paused again. "Yes. I think it will be an interesting experiment. The real hard work comes after that. I also want you to start thinking about visiting JoJo. I think it could really help you."

My heart started to race at the thought of seeing my brother. "Let's try the punching bag first."

CHAPTER FIVE

EL BUHO

The first thing I remember about the gym was the smell. It was bad. The combination of sweat and deodorant made me feel sick. But I wasn't going to be there long. All I wanted to do was see if I could buy a used punching bag.

We didn't have enough money to buy a new one. So my father gave me what little extra he had. Then he sent me over to the Rock River Police Athletic League Boxing Club next to the lumberyard on Railroad Avenue. It was a tiny, concrete structure that used to house a printing company. The presses had been moved out in favor of a boxing ring. Surrounding the ring were several punching bags, big and small. They hung from the low ceiling by metal chains.

After I got past the smell, I focused on the sounds: a passing freight train, loud music from several different boom boxes, and loud grunting. It was a combination of violent shakes, piercing whistles, and salsa and hip-hop beats.

Standing inside the door of the gym, I looked around. On the walls were fight posters. Some of them looked pretty old. Not that I would have recognized the fighters' names anyway. Although I would catch an occasional fight on television, I didn't follow boxing. My one year of youth baseball was cut short when I was kicked off the team for fighting. The same thing happened when I went out for football. So I stopped paying attention to sports.

I stood there waiting to be noticed, watching several dozen people do their thing. Some shadowboxed in front of the mirror. Others jumped rope. A few more hit the punching bags. I soaked it all in. I had never been in a place like this before.

I watched as a pair of teenagers slugged it out in the ring. They didn't move like the pros on television. They looked awkward. I remember thinking that I could do what they were doing. I could beat the two of them easily.

When the bell rang, and the fight was over, the two boxers hugged. Weren't they just trying to knock each other out? Why would they hug? They seemed to have some sort of respect for one another. This display of sportsmanship was unfamiliar to me. I didn't understand it.

Just then, a Hispanic man in his mid-forties with

a thin mustache approached me. I stared closely at him as he sized me up. About five feet ten, he was dressed in sneakers and a black sweat suit. He was balding slightly, and his nose looked as though it had been broken. He had a stopwatch hanging around his neck and a towel draped over his shoulder. He wasn't big, but he was rock hard. It didn't look like he had an ounce of fat on him. There was no question he belonged in a place like this. In fact, he looked like he could take on anyone in the gym.

"Que pasa, amigo?" he said. "Can I help you with something?"

"Si," I said. "I'm here to buy a punching bag."

"Is that so?" responded the man. "This isn't a sporting goods store, chico."

"I know that," I said harshly. "Don't you have a beat-up bag that you don't want anymore?"

"All our bags are beat up," he answered. "That's the way they're supposed to be. People come in here to hit them."

I remember thinking how much of a wise-guy he was. How his sarcastic comments sounded like things I would say. But I didn't admire him for it. I disliked him for putting me off. I muttered something under my breath before turning to leave.

"Did you say something?" he asked, taking a step toward me.

"Not to you," I responded rudely.

The man's lips curled into a small smile. I

couldn't figure out why. He couldn't have liked my tone of voice. "I thought I heard you say something, chico," he said. "But if you tell me you didn't, then you didn't." The man crossed his arms in a confident way.

"I didn't," I repeated.

"Say, why do you want to buy a used punching bag anyway?" the man asked.

"What do you care?" I said. "You're not going to sell me one."

"Es verdad. That's true," said the man. "I was just curious. But if you're afraid to tell me, that's alright."

"I'm not afraid, man," I said, starting to get angry. I wondered why this guy seemed to be provoking me. "You want to know why?" I said. "I want a bag so I can hit it rather than the side of someone's face." I said what I did for shock value, but it was somewhat true. Hearing it come out of my mouth, though, made me raise an eyebrow. I realized how vicious it sounded. I expected a similar response from the man. But he didn't seem fazed by my comment. He just stood there. I looked at him for what seemed like forever. I waited for him to say something. When it appeared he wasn't going to, I turned once again to leave.

"You a tough guy?" he asked.

I turned back around yet again. "Tough enough," I said. I sensed that el fuego wanted to make an appearance. Before I knew it, my hands had balled into fists.

"Then why don't you join the gym, tough guy?" The man had obviously noticed my change in posture. "You can hit your punching bag here."

"I don't want to join this stinkin' gym," I said. I had tried sports before, and it didn't take me long to realize I wasn't a joiner.

"We've got speed bags for hand-eye coordination. We've got double-end bags for practicing defense. And we've got heavy bags for banging," the man said. He pointed to the various bags hanging all over the gym. "If you're really looking to hit something, I recommend the heavy bag."

"I'm not joining your gym," I said. "If you don't have a bag to sell to me, then I'm done here."

"I'll tell you what, hothead," the man said. His tone of voice was becoming stern. He inched closer to me. My eyes came up to his chest, which was rock solid. "My name is Felix Castillo. I'm the head trainer and manager here at the PAL," he said. "You come here and paint that wall over there, and I'll *give* you a heavy bag. No charge. Think you can handle that?"

I looked over at the wall he was referring to. It was in need of a fresh coat of paint. A couple of days after school, helping this guy, and I'd have a heavy bag. I knew my dad and Dr. Colòn wouldn't let up until I did something. Maybe hitting a bag was just the medicine I needed.

I didn't like Mr. Castillo one bit. But it seemed like a fair enough deal. I unclamped my fists. "Okay, Señor," I said. "You got it."

"Muy bien," he said. "What's your name?"

"Paco Diaz," I answered.

"Be here tomorrow at four o'clock, Diaz," said Felix Castillo. "And be on time."

Señor Castillo was waiting for me the following day. He held a paint brush, several buckets of paint and a drop cloth. "You're late," he said.

I looked up at the clock on the wall. It read three minutes past the hour. "It's only a few minutes after four," I said.

"Like I said, you're late," Mr. Castillo said. "Here's everything you need, except a ladder. You'll find one in the storage closet over there. Have fun."

I watched Felix Castillo climb into the ring to demonstrate some moves to a kid he was training. He saw me out of the corner of his eye. "Hey, Diaz!" he shouted. "You here to watch boxing or paint my wall?"

I turned back to my task. I once again muttered to myself how much of a jerk this guy was.

I was back at the PAL the next day and the day after that. I worked hard all three afternoons. But I did catch everything that was going on around me. One afternoon, there was a heavyweight hitting the bag with such power that it was frightening. It was also really cool to watch. The next day, it was a group of middleweights shadowboxing. They were so intense. They looked like they were actually fighting.

It was difficult painting in the middle of this place. I realized I was witnessing something that not too many people get to see. All I knew about boxing up until that point was what you see on television: "Tonight, the championship bout, live from Las Vegas." It's all very colorful. The participants and the paying guests look their best. And there are always celebrities who show up to be seen at ringside. The boxing I knew about was like a circus.

What I was experiencing here was the opposite. This was the side of boxing the public never saw. I was witnessing the grit and grime associated with a bunch of dreamers. Each of these wannabes thought that, one day, they'd be able to fight under the bright lights.

In the PAL gym, the only things colorful were the characters who inhabited it. The gym was small, crowded, and windowless. Even the men's room had no view of the world outside. Simply put, this place was a dump. It was a different world, all right, and one I didn't want to be part of. Besides, my work was done. It was time to go.

After putting the finishing touches on my masterpiece, I spotted El Buho. That's Spanish for The Owl. It's what I heard a few of the boxers call Coach Castillo. At the moment, he was shouting instructions in Spanish from alongside the ring. "La derecha, la derecha," he yelled. "Throw the right hand."

I approached him from behind. "I finished the job," I said. "Now, which bag is mine?"

Coach Castillo turned to face me. It was obviously he wasn't thrilled about having been interrupted. "You're not done yet," he said, turning around to watch the action in the ring.

"What do you mean?" I answered. "I just finished."

"Two coats?" he said, still watching the sparring session.

"You never said anything about two coats?" I answered. I could feel my blood starting to boil. I was convinced this guy was doing everything he could to set me off. On the other hand, I was doing everything I could to remain calm.

"Everybody knows a wall needs two coats," said El Buho.

Once again, I felt my hands turn into fists. Señor Castillo must have sensed it, because he immediately turned around. "Two coats, Diaz, or no bag," he said. "That's the deal!"

I felt like hitting him. I think he knew it, too. Right then and there, I knew that el fuego had been lit. At least I had enough sense to walk away, back toward the wall. But I wasn't okay. Not yet. Passing by one of the gym's heavy bags, I took a swing. I nailed it with my right hand. Although it didn't move much, the sound my fist made hitting it was loud. It was a good sound, and I wanted to hear it again. And again.

Next thing I knew, I was flailing away on that bag. I was firing lefts and rights until my knuckles were raw. The feeling I got when I hit that bag was something I'll never forget. All the energy in my body had been released. And I honestly felt at peace. Either that, or I was simply too exhausted to be angry. Stopping and dropping my hands to my side, I stood there huffing and puffing. I glanced over my shoulder. El Buho was staring at me. "Not bad," he said. "You're really fast, chico. But you're doing it all wrong."

I was too tired to tell him to go stuff it! Besides, el fuego seemed to have been extinguished.

"Hands hurt a little, don't they?" El Buho asked.

Boy, did they ever! But I wasn't about to tell him that. I didn't answer.

"I have an idea, Diaz," he said, walking over to me. "How would you like to learn how to box?"

"I know how to fight," I said between wheezes.

"I didn't say fight. Fighting is an entirely different activity. I asked if you'd like to learn how to box."

I wasn't quick enough to ask him why. I just figured he didn't like the way I was punching the bag. I thought he wanted to let me know I wasn't anything special. "No," I said. I would have to be crazy to come here and put up with The Owl.

"That's too bad," Señor Castillo said. I thought our conversation would end right there, but he wasn't giving up yet. "I'll tell you what. I'll give you a choice."

"What choice?" I responded.

"You finish the second coat and, like we agreed, you take a bag home," he said. "That will give you something to bang away at when you're mad. Now, that's okay. But you start hitting that thing the wrong way and you could do serious damage. I've seen it happen."

"Is that right?" I was suddenly more interested in the sport he was so obviously selling.

"Your other choice is that you come here and do the same thing—the right way. It's the one I recommend you take. In the process, you'll learn how to box. It's up to you," he concluded.

I thought for a second. I had participated in a bunch of activities in my life, but none satisfied me. Why would this be any different? Then, I looked over at that heavy bag again. The truth was, I loved hitting that bag. The rush I got as I unleashed punch after punch was unmatched. I wanted more. But I didn't like the idea of injuring myself because I wasn't punching correctly. Not only my knuckles—but my wrists—felt the sting. Even my right shoulder ached.

Until I got el fuego under control, I was going to need my fists. Even more pressing was my need to get Dad and Dr. Colòn off my back. "All right, Señor Castillo," I said. "I'll come to the gym for a few lessons."

"Good," he said. "But first you have to apply that second coat."

CHAPTER SIX

FIRE DOWN BELOW

My dad had been a good athlete in his day. He was a second baseman on his high school baseball team back home. Dad was good enough to be invited to try out with the Mayaguez Indians. They've won fifteen Puerto Rican League championships and two Caribbean World Series. So I guess I had some athletic genes in my body.

According to my dad, this boxing experiment was a worthwhile one. He talked to me about what I would learn through boxing—discipline, dedication, and self-control. Learning how to box, thanks to a Puerto Rican former fighter, was a bonus.

My mom wasn't quite so sure. She thought boxing was the most brutal of sports. How was this going to help me learn to be less violent? Mom didn't see it. She made a strong argument against me participating. Everything she said made sense.

Truthfully, Dr. Colòn wasn't excited about it either. During our next session, she told me some of her concerns. I'm not sure why, but I defended the sport I barely knew anything about. I spoke calmly, but with passion. "The guy at the gym says boxing and fighting aren't the same. He says boxing is a sport. It's all about self-control, which is just what you and I were talking about. I can't pretend I don't have the killer instinct. I have to deal with it, right?"

"I don't know, Paco," said Dr. Colòn. "I wanted you to find a release for your anger so as not to fight. I don't know if regularly being surrounded by violence is good for you. I'm not going to say you can't do it, though," she added. "Not yet at least."

It was Thursday and a school holiday. I finished painting that second coat the day before. My dad had taken a half day off from work. He wanted to bring me to my first workout at the PAL. On the drive over, I thought about what El Buho had said. Boxing and fighting weren't the same thing. I wasn't sure if I actually believed him.

I also wondered if I would be a good boxer. I have to admit, I was pretty nervous about performing well. Sure, I had done a lot of fighting in my twelve years. But if Coach Castillo was right, then, would I be any good at boxing? The fighting I had engaged in didn't have any rules. I would kick, pull hair, and bite—

whatever it took. I assumed the sport of boxing had a bunch of rules. Not only did I have to follow them, I had to do so while fighting. I could see how this would be difficult. I would have to control myself during the peak of el fuego's fury. This test, as Dr. Colòn called it, was going to be interesting.

"Diaz!" El Buho shouted as my father and I walked through the front door of the gym "What are you waiting for?" He pointed to the door to my left. "Go in the bathroom and get changed."

I trotted off toward the men's room with my gym bag. I looked back to see him shaking hands with my dad. "Señor Diaz, mucho gusto," said El Buho.

"Coach Castillo," my dad replied. "The pleasure is mine."

El Buho smiled. "Your son has a fire in his belly, no?"

"Si," my dad said. "Only it's in his head, too. And it clouds his judgment."

"I think coming here will be a good thing for Paco, no?" said Coach Castillo.

"I wouldn't be here if I didn't think so," my dad said.

I changed as quickly as I could. I didn't want to give my father and El Buho too much time together. One thing I could be thankful for was having spent those days painting the wall. As a result, I was somewhat used to the horrible smell of the gym. After I had spent five minutes in the men's room, the smell settled into my nostrils. Being there then became a bit more bearable.

Exiting the men's room, I saw that El Buho was no longer with my dad. I spotted him in the doorway of the one room next to the ring. I figured it was his office. He was busy talking to a young boxer. The kid was dressed in blue and gold trunks and a gold tank top. On his feet were brilliant white boxing shoes. I glanced down at my wardrobe. I wore a faded blue t-shirt and gray gym shorts. On my feet were high-top canvas sneakers. The sneaks were my dad's. He wore them to do work around the apartment. They were once black. Now they were speckled with white spots from painting the kitchen last summer. They were certainly better than my everyday sneakers. According to my father, his shoes would at least give me some ankle support.

When I asked for a pair of boxing shoes, my dad laughed. He then looked at me sternly. "Let's see if you stick it out before I run off and buy boxing shoes." Although his words were not a vote of confidence, they made sense. I didn't know what to make of boxing. Besides, I had been thrown off every team I'd ever played on. I had quit almost everything I'd ever tried. I'm sure Dad feared this wouldn't be any different.

Checking out the rest of the gym, I saw boxers of all shapes and sizes. They were sparring, shadowboxing, hitting the bags and jumping rope. There were about thirty boxers in all crammed into the Rock River PAL Boxing Club. And it was only two o'clock in the afternoon.

At least I wasn't the only kid in the place. In fact, there were several boxers even younger than me. Two were in the ring at that moment. Spanish was the language you heard above the boxers' grunts and growls. The two trainers watching the pair in the ring were the loudest. They screamed and yelled the whole time.

Just then, the sight of Felix Castillo heading my way interrupted my thoughts. "Diaz!" he shouted, brushing past my dad. "Ven aca. Come over here." As I started to make my way toward him, I glanced over at my dad. He just looked at me and smiled. It was like he knew something I didn't. Then, he turned and left. I was on my own.

About thirty minutes later, I was groaning my way through my third set of sit-ups. According to Felix Castillo, my job was simple: I was to do everything he told me to do. I was not to ask questions. Those were the rules of our unwritten contract. In return, he would teach me how to box. Obviously, I didn't like the deal. I couldn't recall signing any working papers.

At first, the physical suffering was almost too much to bear. I didn't feel like I ever got into a rhythm. And yet, the painful burn masked the fact that my muscles were loosening and stretching. I had never really done much in the way of exercise. So this was new to me. And my efforts felt anything but good— especially with El Buho shouting at me.

After the sit-ups, it was on to push-ups, and then leg stretches. Over an hour had gone by, and I hadn't even laced on gloves. I was in pain, and I was tired of Coach Castillo barking at me. "Push it, Diaz! Push it! C'mon, now!"

All the while, El Buho told me to focus on my breathing. He said it was necessary to build my stamina and endurance. I didn't know what he was talking about.

A few minutes later, he told me to stand up and watch him closely. I was beginning to see red. I could sense el fuego coming. El Buho proceeded to show me exactly how he wanted me to skip rope. He then threw the rope to me and told me to get to it. That's when I broke our pact. I dropped the rope, officially signaling the end to my workout.

"I didn't call time!" yelled Coach Castillo.

"That's okay," I said. "I did."

"You don't get to do that," said El Buho. The anger in his voice could be heard across the gym. "That's my job! Your job is to do what I say!"

"Save it for one of these other guys," I said. I turned to walk away. As I did, I remember thinking that Dr. Colòn would be happy. My father, on the other hand, would be mad—really mad. I was suddenly glad he hadn't bought me those shoes. I wanted out.

El Buho was yelling at me to stop, but I kept walking. As I did, one of the other boxers approached me. He was a few years older than I was. But I had never seen him before. I turned to face him, wondering who he was and what he wanted. He started yelling. "You know that teacher you bit in the playground, you little punk?" He pushed me backward. "That was my grandfather. Let's go outside so I can teach you what it feels like to be attacked."

It didn't matter that I knew I was wrong to bite Señor Bermudez. I should have admired his grandson for sticking up for him, too. But I didn't. Looking at this guy, my eyes narrowed. The fury that had already been building inside me suddenly peaked. It even caught me by surprise—not to mention Coach Castillo.

Before Señor Bermudez' grandson opened his mouth again, I was all over him. I remember hitting him with a hook to the abdomen that took his breath away. It was a short, fast and direct punch, thrown correctly from my side. It was a punch I didn't even know I was capable of throwing effectively. It was apparently a textbook shot.

As he stood there frozen, I noticed his hands at his sides. I then nailed him in the face with a straight right hand. By then, Coach Castillo had caught up to me. He wrapped his arms around my chest and pulled me off. Several others stood over my victim, who had slumped to the ground. They were helping him to his feet. He started yelling. I tried to get at him through El Buho's arms. I was enraged, lost somewhere between reality and my own sense of justice. Deep down, though, I didn't want to fight. But I was in that place again, where el fuego blazed. When I was there, nothing else mattered.

Coach Castillo was able to hold me back. As I started to calm down, I began thinking: this would make my dad mad, yes. Even worse, it would mean writing my ticket to military school. I had been at the gym only one day. Already I was going to be forced to pack up my things and never return.

That's not what happened, though. I was told to wait while Coach Castillo spoke quietly to Señor Bermudez's grandson. Then El Buho walked over to me. He looked mad. His face was flushed red as he spoke. "You want to fight someone, Diaz?" The veins in his neck bulged. "Fight me, then, chico."

I stood there staring at the ground, then back up at El Buho. I returned my gaze to the ground. I didn't know what to do. I certainly didn't want to fight The Owl.

"That guy started it," I said nervously. "You saw him challenge me. He pushed me and—"

"We do not fight in this gym unless it's in there," said El Buho, pointing toward the ring. "If you want to fight so badly, then you and I can do it in there." He sounded serious.

"I'm just a kid," I responded.

"Then it shouldn't take me long," said El Buho, now inches from my face. He tossed me a pair of boxing gloves and stepped between the ropes. "Come inside, tough guy. You've been waiting to punch all night." He threw four or five hard punches into the air.

I was speechless. I never met anyone like him before. I didn't know how to react to his behavior. I certainly didn't want to step into the ring with him. Thankfully, after several seconds, I didn't have to. "Okay. I see you don't want to fight," he said. "Then dig this, and dig it good." He removed his boxing gloves and tossed them aside. "You don't change your attitude, chico, you're going to end up behind bars."

"So what if I do," I said. "I can handle it."

"You think doing time is easy?" El Buho asked. He was shouting now. "You think it's no big deal? You think you're so tough you could handle it? You don't know anything, chico."

"I know enough," I said.

El Buho turned his head away from me. "Henry," he said to one of the other trainers, another Puerto Rican. "I have to leave for a while. You're in charge." Henry nodded, as did several other trainers and boxers. A few of them smirked as well.

"You'll be gone a couple of hours, right, capitan?"

"Si," said El Buho. "No mas."

That's when he took me on a road trip.

CHAPTER SEVEN

THERAPY

Before I knew it, El Buho had dragged me out-side. He dumped me into the front seat of his pickup truck. After making me strap on my seatbelt, he made a call on his cell phone. Then, he got in and started the engine.

"This is kidnapping," I said to him as he pulled away.

"So take me to court," Coach Castillo said, looking straight ahead.

This guy was something else, I thought. I didn't know what to say to El Buho. Nor was I interested in having a conversation with him. So I watched the scen-ery pass by me through the front seat window. I did wonder where we were headed, however.

After a half hour, we arrived at our destination: the State Correctional Institution at Graterford. I knew right away that I was going to be taught a lesson. The jail, Pennsylvania's largest maximum-security prison, was imposing from a distance. Looking up at it from just outside the front gate was downright terrifying.

Everywhere you looked, there were bars. There were bars on the windows, bars on the doors, bars on the bars. In addition to the bars were coiled razor wire, steel security doors, and metal detectors. They didn't call it maximum security for nothing.

"Let's go, Diaz," said El Buho. "I want you to meet someone."

My heart began racing. Coach Castillo didn't know what I had been thinking about. It entered my head the moment I saw the prison on the horizon. JoJo, my brother, whom I hadn't seen in four years, was here. He had been transferred to Graterford on his eighteenth birthday. How could El Buho know that, I wondered. Did he know that? Was he going to introduce me to my own brother? Thousands of questions filled my brain as a brawny black corrections officer approached the truck.

"El Buho Castillo!" the guard called out. "Que pasa, mi amigo?"

"Billy Reed!" said Coach Castillo. "Thanks for seeing me on such short notice." The two men shook hands.

"Paco Diaz, this is Bad Billy Reed. He's one of the best amateur boxers to ever come out of Philly," said El Buho. "And Billy, this is Paco Diaz. He's a punk kid who just thinks he's bad."

The guard looked like he could still go a few rounds. He smiled. "Time to go to school, son," he said. I stepped out of the car and followed him. As we walked through the front door of the prison, I took a whiff. It smelled a little better than the Rock River PAL, but not much. And it definitely wasn't an inviting place. In fact, everything about it was horrible.

"Ready for a tour?" Billy Reed asked me.

"Do I have a choice?"

Billy chuckled. Then he turned to El Buho. "You're right—this kid does need a lesson."

Bad Billy Reed escorted me through a large metal door. When I had passed through, I turned back to El Buho. "Aren't you coming?"

"I've seen it before," he responded with a smile.

Our first stop on the tour was Cell Block D. I didn't know what to expect. But the look on Billy Reed's face said it was going to be eye-opening. We turned the corner into a huge room. It seemed longer than a football field. Prison cells lined both walls, two stories high. We stood at the end of the hallway. Billy told me the residents called it Broadway, after the famous street in New York. It was where convicts gathered several times a day to be counted.

Billy whispered to me. Recently, an inmate had been killed by a rival gang member on Broadway. I gulped loudly. "Let's go," Billy said, taking a step down the center aisle, between the cells.

"Where?" I asked.

He pointed to the far end of the cell block.

"Down there?" I gulped.

"Yup."

"You're kidding, right?" I said nervously. Then I stopped walking. "Listen, I get the point. Prison stinks."

"Not yet you don't. Walk with me, son, or you can stay here alone." Billy kept going. "You don't follow me down this hall, you can't get out of here." Then he pointed at the prisoners. "In fifteen minutes, it's dinner time. Then these doors open up. I wouldn't want to be standing there alone if I were you."

Just as those words escaped his lips, a prisoner screamed. "You can leave him here with me!"

I started walking as fast as I could toward Billy. My entire body was shaking. Once I caught up with him, we began to stroll down Broadway. I kept my eyes focused on the far wall, at the end of the room. I didn't want to make eye contact with any of the inmates. I could feel them staring at me.

"Fresh meat!" one convict yelled.

"Fresh meat!" shouted another.

Within seconds, the entire cell block was yelling "Fresh meat." The sound was deafening. Every time I heard another voice scream those words, I flinched.

Several of the convicts spit in my direction. Although I was in the middle of the corridor, I wasn't out of harm's way. Some of the inmates, especially those on the second tier, were great spitters. They were skilled at hitting me on the chest, back, and side of my head. Although he was walking right next to me, Billy Reed was dry as a bone.

They were doing anything and everything they could to get me to look at them. I refused. The truth was, I was too scared. The end of Broadway seemed like it was in Canada. I didn't know if I could make it all the way.

"Open Number Seventy-two!" yelled Billy. A guard was sitting in a caged office at the opposite end of the room. He punched a few keys on his computer, and one of the cells opened automatically. Out stepped a hulking, bald, Hispanic inmate. He was dressed in standard prison attire: navy blue hospital scrubs. He had cut off his short sleeves to show off his tattoos. One was on his enormous right arm. His left displayed even more colorful artwork. There, the ink covered every inch of his skin from his wrist to his shoulder. Around his neck was a tattoo of barbed wire.

"Inmate Number 48642!" called Billy. "Take a walk on Broadway!"

The largest man I had ever seen in my life walked up to me. He neither extended his hand nor spoke. He just walked alongside me, looking straight ahead.

"Antonio," said Billy Reed. "Tell this boy about the joint."

The inmate glanced down at me. I felt a shiver

run down my spine. He turned his gaze back to the front. "You've got to mentally prepare yourself for a place like this," he said slowly. He wanted to make sure I listened to every word he said. It was hard, with all the shouting going on. But I heard him loud and clear. "You have to—especially for that first day. Within your first hour here, you'll be strip-searched, hosed down, and dressed like me. Then you'll have your life threatened by some pretty hard dudes."

I tried to swallow the lump that was forming in my throat. But I couldn't. Just then, a rat scampered across Broadway directly in front of us. I shuddered. As it ran, the residents of Cell Block D let out a collective cheer.

"Prison is a stressful place, hermano," said Antonio. "You're getting a gift today, and you don't even know it. This little preview will keep you from being as shocked when you join us for real."

I glanced over at Bad Billy Reed. He was just walking, taking it all in.

"Once you get here, you can't act out," Antonio went on. "If you do, the guards will label you a troublemaker. Then, you'll be subjected to a world of hurt. They can make your life miserable." He looked into my eyes for the first time. "You're not a troublemaker, are you, boy?"

I shook my head no. Antonio grunted his disbelief.

"Good, because you want to keep a low profile in here. Remember, prison is full of predators."

At that point, he stopped. So did Billy. I hadn't realized it, but we had walked the entire length of Broadway. Antonio looked down at me once more. "Anything else you want to know?"

Again, I shook my head from side to side. Billy started to push me toward the exit. The other guard came out of the office to usher Antonio back to his cell. "Hey, don't you want to know what I'm in here for?" he asked.

"No," I said, finally able to speak. I quickly let the door close behind me. I had already seen enough of prison to know that I didn't want to end up there.

Plus, I had managed to walk through Graterford without coming across JoJo. I don't think I breathed the whole time I was there. I was scared of what I was seeing. But I was terrified about the possibility of bumping into my brother. I didn't know what I would do or say. I wanted to get out of there before it happened.

Within minutes, we were back in the lobby. El Buho was waiting for us. He was talking to a couple of officers who seemed to know him well. I wondered if they were ex-boxers, too. As Bad Billy Reed stuck out his hand to me. I shook it. "I hope I never see you here," he said.

He and El Buho hugged before the trainer and I headed for the parking lot. Once I was sitting in the truck, I breathed a sigh of relief. El Buho didn't really know why. He thought it was because of what I had just experienced. He didn't know about my brother.

I looked through the window toward the prison one last time before leaving. That's when I saw him in the exercise yard. JoJo was standing between a black prisoner and a Hispanic. He was much bigger than I remembered. And it wasn't only because four years had gone by. It was obvious he spent quite a few afternoons in the courtyard lifting weights. I couldn't blame him. The place he lived in was the scariest place in the world.

Even though we were about two hundred yards away, I had no doubt about it: That face was my brother's. I was sure our eyes met, just as El Buho stepped on the gas and pulled away.

CHAPTER EIGHT

THE VISIT

That night, at home, I couldn't focus. Not during dinner when my dad asked me about my first day at the gym. Not while I was doing my homework. I couldn't stop seeing JoJo in my head. His eyes, his huge frame, the look on his face, it all haunted me. Not to mention the thought of him in prison. I felt terrible for him.

Lying in bed, I stared at the wall. This was the same room I used to share with JoJo. I remembered a time when JoJo slept right there against that wall. Although his bed had long since been removed, I still imagined him asleep there some nights.

"What's bothering you, Paco?" my mom asked as she entered my room. She must have known I wasn't asleep. She put her hand on my shoulder. "You're not yourself tonight. No dinner. No television."

"Did something happen at the gym?" my dad asked sternly. He stood in the doorway. "Don't tell me you're ready to quit already, because—"

I cut him off before he began to yell. "I'm not quitting," I said.

"Look, Paco," he replied, his voice getting louder. "I expect you to stick with boxing. You made a commitment to Señor Castillo, and I expect you to honor it. Comprende?"

"Si, papa," I answered. But I wasn't thinking about boxing or El Buho. I was thinking about the State Correctional Institution at Graterford. I was thinking about JoJo. But I couldn't tell my father that. Thankfully, he shut the lights and they left the room. I wasn't about to fall asleep, but I closed my eyes. I thought about how JoJo and I made eye contact earlier that day. I wondered if he was lying in his bed, thinking about me, too. That night, all my dreams were about my brother.

The next morning, I knew what I had to do. The only problem was figuring out how I would get back to Graterford. Walking to school, I came up with a plan. I would ask Felix Castillo for help. After all, he caused this problem.

All day in school, I couldn't wait for the bell to ring. Finally, it was three o'clock. I bolted down the front steps of St. Joe's and ran as fast as I could to the Rock River PAL. Crashing through the front door,

I looked up to see El Buho. He was staring at me from inside his office. "I didn't think you'd be back today," he said. "I'm impressed, Diaz."

"I'm not here to train today," I said. "I need a favor."

"You do?" said El Buho. "I didn't know we knew each other well enough to start asking for favors. What can I do for you?"

"Can you drive me back to Graterford this afternoon," I said.

El Buho looked confused. "Why, chico?"

"I'll tell you on the way."

For the next half-hour, I explained it all to El Buho. I told him about my brother and my killer instinct. And how my psychologist wanted me to visit him. I told him I hadn't even thought about it until the day before. And I told him it was his duty to take me back to Graterford.

I left out two things. One, that Dr. Colón really didn't want me to box. And, two, I wasn't sure if I wanted to do it, either. While I talked, El Buho drove. He didn't say anything. He didn't pass judgment. He just listened. He didn't even say I owed him one for agreeing to drive me.

When we arrived, Coach Castillo went to visit with Billy Reed. I went to see JoJo. As we parted, El Buho wished me luck. I needed it. Fifteen minutes later, I was sitting in a strange room on an uncomfortable plastic chair. I was behind six inches of soundproof glass. I waited for my brother to arrive.

My heart pounded inside my chest. I wondered if JoJo would look as broken as the other men I had seen there. I wondered what he would say to me. He didn't know that I had come to see him. The only thing the guards told him was that he had a visitor. I was as unsure about this meeting as anything else in my life. Would my brother even want to see me?

Just then, the door on the far wall opened. In walked a burly guard followed by a young Latino. It was the same Latino I saw the day before—the same Latino who grew up sleeping five feet away from me. Sadly, though, JoJo looked sullen. It wasn't the happy face he used to have as a teenager. Back then, it didn't take much to make him smile and laugh.

As soon as his eyes met mine, they came alive. So did his mouth. He grinned from ear to ear. I grinned, too. Sitting, he picked up a telephone receiver on his side of the glass. He indicated to me with his hands that I should do the same. "Paco," he said, choking up a bit. "It was you yesterday. I knew it."

"Yeah," I said. My eyes started to fill up with tears.

"Listen to your voice." JoJo closed his eyes. "Man, just the way I remember it."

I smiled. "You sound the same, too."

"Sometimes when I close my eyes at night, I hear that voice." JoJo rubbed his eyes, trying hard to contain his tears. "It's good to see you, hermano."

He took a deep breath. "So what were you doing here yesterday?" he asked.

"It was like a school trip," I said, lying.

"You weren't here to see me," he said. "But you changed your mind when we spotted each other."

"Something like that," I said sheepishly. "I was scared."

JoJo seemed to be deep in thought. "You're here now."

"Si," I said.

"Man, you got big," he said, looking me over.

"So did you," I replied.

"Not much else to do in here," he said, flexing his right bicep.

Just then—from out of nowhere—I felt el fuego rumble inside me. "You could have written me a letter or two, JoJo." I spoke with force behind each word.

"I wrote you a hundred," he answered. "But I ripped them all up before mailing them."

"Why?"

"You don't understand what it's like in here, Paco. You start to question yourself. Do I deserve a family? Do I deserve a brother? A lot of times, the answer I came up with was no. I'd start writing and then think you were better off without me in your life. I'm so ashamed of what I've done. I didn't know how to tell you how sorry I was."

JoJo looked down at his feet for a few moments. I thought about what he had just said.

It seemed like an eternity before I spoke. I did everything I could to stop myself from crying. "You were my best friend." I put my fist up against the glass that separated us.

JoJo put his fist up across from mine and banged on the glass lightly. "Why'd it take you so long to come and see me then? I've missed you, bro."

"I missed you, too. For a long time, I hated you for what you did," I said. "I hated you for committing the crime. But I hated you even more for leaving me. Dad would never let me come here either. He doesn't know I'm here now. We don't even mention your name at home."

JoJo hung his head.

"Seeing you makes me feel better, though, 'cause I still need my brother," I said.

"Good," JoJo said, smiling. "I need my brother, too." Our eyes locked on one another. I knew right then that JoJo would be a part of my future. To be honest, it was the greatest feeling I had felt in years.

He continued. "I know I messed up, Paco. I know I hurt a lot of people, especially my family. I can't take back what I've done," he said. "I can only tell you that not a day goes by that I don't regret it. I'm paying the price, Paco. I've lost a lot. I don't want to lose you again."

I didn't know what to say. I was still hurt, and I was still angry. But I wanted nothing more than to reach out and hug my brother. I knew right away that coming to see him was the right thing. It felt good to know he existed again.

After that, we just sat there a while. We'd look at each other and then down at our shoes. JoJo broke the silence. "So what have you been up to?"

I answered him right away. "I'm boxing," I said. "I mean, I'm just starting, but I like it." These words actually surprised me. I guess I really did like boxing. "I had my first training session at the PAL last night." I added.

"You're going to be a boxer?"

"I don't know," I said. "I've got some problems with my temper. Mom and Dad are making me see a psychologist. I'm only going so Dad doesn't send me to military school," I continued. "I don't know if I even have what it takes to box. I'm not really into sports, you know. And my trainer is a real burro."

"Paco, listen to me. The biggest mistake I made was not getting involved in something. I didn't join the PAL, or the football team, or the baseball team. I joined a gang. So, instead of hitting a home run or scoring the winning touchdown, I'm here, in prison. If you've got anger issues, Paco, all the more reason you need to stick with something like boxing. I wish I had," he added. "You let your anger get the best of you, and you'll end up like me."

I looked at my brother. I didn't want to end up in prison. I didn't want my anger to control me any longer.

"Diaz!" yelled a guard, interrupting my thoughts. "Time to say goodbye."

"I gotta go, bro," JoJo said. "Thanks for coming. It means everything to me."

"Me, too," I responded.

"Stick with the boxing, Paco," he said. "Then come back soon and tell me all about it."

That Monday's session with Dr. Colòn went pretty well. She was happy about my progress. And it felt good.

"You saw your brother?" she asked in disbelief. "That's wonderful, Paco. But I didn't think you felt ready to do that."

"It kind of just happened," I said.

"I'm proud of you," she said. "I'm surprised, too. Do you feel like talking about it?"

"Believe it or not, I do," I said, grinning. "I also want to tell you that I'm going to give this boxing thing a shot. Even though I know you're against it."

"Well, you caught me off guard with your visit to JoJo," she said. "I'm willing to see if you've got any more surprises up your sleeve."

The next day, El Buho told me he would tape my hands in his office.

"What gives?" I said. "I don't want any special treatment."

"Trust me, Diaz, you won't get any," El Buho

said. "I just wanted to tell you something. You know the guy you punched out the other night, Elmer Bermudez?"

"I do now," I said.

"Well, he's waiting for you over by the bathroom," Coach Castillo said. "Go shake his hand, then come right back here."

I walked over to Elmer Bermudez and extended my hand to him. It was something I couldn't recall ever doing before. It was a weird feeling, but not a bad one. He returned the shake. Neither of us spoke nor even looked at each other. But, as far as we were concerned, the matter was closed. The fact that I was able to do that, made me feel like I was making progress. I was taming el fuego. A few days ago, I'd never have shaken hands with someone I had recently fought.

When I returned to his office, Coach Castillo was behind his desk. He was sitting beneath a number of photos, mostly of Rock River PAL boxers. One showed a young Felix El Buho Castillo. He was holding up his gold medal from the 1975 National Police Athletic League tournament. "Sit down," said El Buho, offering me the folding chair opposite his desk.

"Listen, Paco," he began. It was the first time he had called me by that name. "We both know that you've got a fire inside you. With some work, it can serve you well in the ring. But if you don't follow my instructions, it could also work against you. It could burn you down, chico."

I nodded.

"Do you realize Elmer is a seasoned boxer six years older than you?" he asked.

I hadn't, until then. I smiled.

"Throwing a lucky punch doesn't make you a boxer," he added. The grin left my face.

"Who says it was lucky?" I shot back.

"I do," said El Buho. "You're out of control, with no sense and certainly no discipline. You bring that into the ring, and you'll lose every time. I don't care how many lucky punches you land. An experienced boxer will get inside your head. Once he's in there, he'll beat you up bad, chico. Real bad."

I made a face. I only half-believed what he was telling me.

"You're a head case, Diaz," El Buho continued. "Your anger has no place in the ring. That's my first job in training you. I need to teach you discipline. Your entire life is going to change. When we're finished, you'll be a boxer. You'll be in total control of your emotions. But it's not going to be easy."

"From this moment forward, you're here to work hard and listen to me," he added. "As long as you do, I'll help you become a better person."

I nodded my head in agreement. But I couldn't help saying, "You and everyone else."

"Well, you've already proven you can't do it on your own," El Buho said. "And that's okay, chico.

There's no shame in accepting help." He leaned in closer to me, looking deep into my eyes. "I can help you get rid of those demons inside of you. Believe me, Paco, I know all about them."

CHAPTER NINE

GROUND RULES

Running next to the train tracks, I dodged broken bottles and garbage. I ran as hard and as fast as I could. All the while, I concentrated on my breathing. I could feel my leg muscles struggle. My chest pounded. Every inch of my body hurt, but I couldn't stop. I wouldn't stop.

Coach Castillo said that "road work can be the most boring part of one's training." He also was quick to point out that it was necessary. It would ensure that I had something left in my tank in the later rounds. I heard his voice in my head as I ran.

I looked down. My dad's sneakers were holding up okay. I wasn't concerned that I would twist an ankle. I was more worried that I'd be late. Coach Castillo said if I was late more than once, I was done.

As part of my training, El Buho wanted me to

run to the gym every day. Except Sunday, which was my day off. He had two Sunday rules. "First, you spend time with your family," he said. "Then, you have your mom make you a steak and some tostones. Got it?"

"I got it," I replied. It's a good thing I liked beef and fried plantains.

I sprinted the last one hundred yards or so, making it with two minutes to spare. I quickly went inside the gym. I hurried over to have my hands taped by one of the trainers.

"Just made it, eh?" asked the elderly trainer, Henry Garcia. He didn't bother to look up. "Estas cansado? You tired, Diaz?"

"A little," I said. "I'll be okay."

"You the kid who punched out Elmer Bermudez the other day?" asked the man. "The same kid who painted that wall over there?"

"Yeah, that's me," I said.

The man started chuckling to himself.

"What's so funny?" I asked.

"Nada," said Henry. "Private joke. I heard all about you. You're the crazy one with the killer instinct. I heard you're totally out of control, no?" he asked in his thick accent.

"What do you know about me?" I asked. He was starting to get under my skin.

"Don't worry about what I know," he said. "Should I be nervous standing near you, chico?" The man smiled in a sarcastic way.

"What do you mean?" I snorted. I didn't like Garcia's tone of voice. I didn't even know who this wrinkled old dude was.

"A killer instinct is used to describe delinquents," Henry said. "Are you one of those criminales?"

"Why do you care?" I asked. I was growing angrier with every passing moment. I could feel el fuego. It was lit. I inched closer to the man. "You scared I might hurt you?" I said with a snarl.

"Scared of you?" responded the seventy-five-year-old trainer. He dropped the tape to look me straight in the eyes. "Nah. You're just a kid with an attitude problem. A punk who got his shrink to make an excuse for him."

That was it. I snapped. Only this time I didn't raise my hands. I chose a less violent, but perhaps an even worse response. I spit in Henry Garcia's face.

It was the same thing that was done to me several days before at Graterford. I certainly didn't appreciate it when it happened to me. Now I was acting like one of the prisoners. Realizing what I had done, I stood up. I expected some type of retaliation. None came. Instead, Henry Garcia reached for a towel and calmly wiped his face. He picked up the tape and looked at me.

I sat back down with a confused look on my face. Having Henry staring at me was uncomfortable. So I did something I don't recall ever doing before. I apologized. "I'm sorry," I said, awkwardly. "I shouldn't have done that. It's just, the things you're saying about me—" I stopped myself.

Henry Garcia crossed me up even further by smiling. I mean, I just spat on this guy and he seemed happy about it! "Muy bien," he said. "You passed the test. You know the difference between right and wrong." He paused to let what he just said sink in. "I was trying to get you to explode, chico, and you did. You still have to work on that. But you apologized," he said again. "Wait here. El Buho wants to talk to you."

Coach Castillo had been watching the entire scene unfold from his office. I was totally confused when he approached. "See? You do realize the difference between right and wrong, Paco." Coach Castillo patted Henry on the back as he moved away. Obviously, the old man had performed his task well. "That apology means you're not a social deviant, or a criminal. Not yet at least," he laughed. "You still have trouble controlling your emotions. But I've seen a lot of young kids like you. We can work on that. If you stick with me, Paco, you won't end up in prison."

"My brother would be happy to hear that," I said.

"And so would your parents, no?"

"Si," I answered.

"Muy bien," said El Buho. "Then, let's get to work."

As I started stretching, I couldn't help but wonder about Felix Castillo. He had no financial interest in helping me. But he seemed intent on doing so anyway. He was obsessed with imposing order on my life and fixing my inner demons. It was all he could talk about. We started spending lots of time together. Truthfully, he was helping me every day. What puzzled me was only that I couldn't figure out why he was doing it. Whatever the reason, I decided I would not let El Buho down.

Training started to take on a routine. I would punch the heavy bag with my left hand 100 times. Then, I'd punch 100 times with my right. Each punch was followed by a shout from El Buho. Sometimes, he'd count the punches out loud, "uno, dos, tres." Other times, he'd yell things like "move your feet!"

He was most vocal when I did my daily push-ups. Even now, if I listen hard enough, I can still hear him screaming at me to push myself. "Hit the ground with your chest, Diaz!" he'd shout. "Earn it! Give me everything you have!"

When I'd finally finish my workout, El Buho would sit me down. He'd tell me how much work we still had left to do. He ended all our sessions the same way, with a short speech. "That was a good workout. I know you can do even better, though," he'd say.

"Remember, Paco," he'd always add. "Keep your head on straight. You're in control, chico. If I hear bad reports it's off to military school for you.

Comprende?"

"Si, yo entiendo," I always answered him the same way—yes, I understand.

"We've got a long way to go, Paco," El Buho would add. "But we're getting there."

CHAPTER TEN

OUT OF CONTROL

I learned early on in my boxing education that motion relieves tension. So I kept shadowboxing as my opponent climbed through the ropes. It was my first amateur fight—a three-rounder. Nearly a full year had passed since I first showed up at the PAL. I was now ready to prove myself against an opponent.

Over the past twelve months, I had been in class: "Boxing 101." My professor, El Buho, started me off with the basics. We worked on my stance—my feet, shoulder width apart, my body, slightly turned. Then, we worked on how to punch correctly. I threw jabs, hooks, and uppercuts. I never knew how important technique was for a boxer.

I practiced over and over again. I concentrated on shifting my weight and extending my arms. I kept my elbow flexed and I snapped my wrist. I pivoted my feet and rotated my hips. It was a lot to remember.

In between his speeches and demonstrations, El Buho taught me how to condition my body. We trained hard, keeping in mind strength, stamina, and speed. Inside the ring, he had me spar with bigger, older, and more experienced amateurs. I was making progress. Occasionally, though, I'd lose my cool. When that happened, I'd lose my form and my poise. And I'd become a lousy boxer.

For the most part, though, I kept my killer instinct in check. I only hoped I'd be able to control el fuego during a real fight.

The ring was proving to be a great place for me to release my energy. El fuego would still often start up, but it spread only rarely. I was getting good grades and keeping out of trouble. Principal Grace was thrilled with my progress. She referred to me as a success story.

I visited JoJo often, with El Buho driving me there. My dad never knew. He was just happy that my new-found sport was keeping me in line. Mom, though, went with me a few times. Seeing her with my brother made me so happy.

My brother was my biggest fan. He wanted to know everything about my boxing. He wanted to know what El Buho was like. What the gym was like. What lacing up a pair of gloves was like. He was living through me, and my visits were the highlight of his life. He only wished he could be ringside to see me fight himself. "Soon enough," I'd tell him, as his first parole hearing drew nearer.

Even Dr. Colòn had become a believer. She became somewhat of a fan, too. She would drop by the gym every now and then to watch me do my thing. I thought of her while staring across the ring at David Godwin, my first opponent. Godwin was a fifteen-year-old veteran of ten amateur bouts. He had won them all. In his short time in the ring, Godwin had built a solid reputation.

I was no longer lanky. After twelve months in the gym, I put on some bulk. I now weighed a solid 112 pounds and was fighting as a flyweight. But I didn't feel strong. I felt nervous. I didn't like the feeling. I hoped that once the bell rang, the knots in my stomach would go away. They did. Only it wasn't because I calmed down. It was because thirty seconds into the fight Godwin tagged me with a right hook that had me seeing stars.

My chin hurt and I was mad. So much so that I disregarded just about everything Coach Castillo had taught me. I unleashed everything I had on Godwin. I threw every punch I could think of. Uppercuts, right hooks, left hooks, jabs. But I was throwing them so wildly that none landed. I was trying to fight Godwin, not box him. And, sure enough, he dodged every blow. When the bell rang, he was standing there smiling. I was completely spent, and he knew it.

I knew I had let my emotions get the best of

me. I had forgotten why Coach Castillo had me do all that road work. In short, I let El Buho down. I was so angry I felt just about ready to quit.

"Ready to quit?" he asked as I sat down on the stool in my corner.

"Are you serious?" I replied between gasps.

"Are you?" he answered back.

I didn't think I could lift my arms for ten seconds, much less four minutes. But I figured there was really only one answer to that question. "No," I responded.

"Muy bien," he answered. "Then, let's get back to the game plan."

Coach Castillo reminded me that my job was to stick and move. I was to keep Godwin off balance, then hit him with a right hand. I glanced over to ringside. There, sitting next to my dad, was Dr. Colòn. I guess she wanted to see if the experiment was working. It was my first real test, and I was in danger of failing. Henry Garcia squeezed a sponge full of water over my head. Coach Castillo stuck my mouthpiece back in my mouth. I stood up so Henry could straighten my headgear. El Buho gave me one last piece of advice before Round Two. "Don't quit," he said.

Ding!

I shuffled forward, trying to conserve the energy I had left. I wanted to force Godwin into making a mistake. But I didn't know if I had enough left to cause him any concern. Godwin, however, still had plenty of fuel. He rushed toward me, picking up where he left off. His goal was to force me into another punching frenzy. Either that, or he'd hit me a few more times on the button.

He came straight at me. I tried to sidestep and hit him at the same time. Only, I didn't move fast enough. I missed with a wild left hook. He caught me with a right just south of my belt line. A bit too far south. It was an illegal low-blow, and the ref saw it. He indicated to Godwin that he was officially warned. The ref then sent him to a neutral corner.

That foul was the worst thing that could have happened. It wasn't just because it knocked the wind out of me. It also caused me to lose my head. I went nuts, just as I had in the previous round—only worse. I unloaded on Godwin. Gone was my game plan and my composure. Gone also was my knowledge of boxing.

I began hitting Godwin with everything I brought with me that night. I used my fists, my elbows, my knees, my head, you name it. When it seemed like I couldn't take it further, I did. I took a swing at the ref, who was trying to stop the fight. It was the only punch I threw all night that landed.

CHAPTER ELEVEN

DANCING

After the fight, I felt awful. I couldn't believe what happened. It had been so long since I acted that way. I was embarrassed. More than anything, though, I was disappointed in myself. Deep down, I knew I could be a great boxer. All I had to do was stay in control. But I simply couldn't do it. Frustrated and exhausted, I slumped down into the corner of the locker room. I buried my face in my hands.

El Buho walked in a moment later. I could tell he was angry with me. After all, I had completely fallen apart in my first bout. He walked toward me with heavy steps. He then sat down next to me on the floor. He didn't speak a word. I knew he was upset. He had worked hard training me for this fight. I wanted to apologize, but I was unable to speak. I couldn't even look him in the eyes.

We sat there, side-by-side, in the corner of the empty locker room. El Buho put his arm on my shoulder and sighed. "What are we gonna do with you, chico?" I was surprised at how calm he was. "Looks like we've got more work to do."

I forced a smile. "Si," I whispered. "I'm really sorr—"

Before I could finish my sentence, El Buho cut me off. "I know, Paco. I know you are." And with that, he stood up and left the room. I sat there in silence for the next hour or so.

On the car ride home, my dad was not as nice. He said I was letting the fire inside burn me to the ground. He said I was blowing an opportunity—maybe my last one. Of course, he mentioned military school again.

A few weeks after the fight, I still felt awful. I regretted losing my cool and hitting the ref. I also didn't like being written about negatively in the local newspaper. It seemed like I had poured a year of training—and psychology—down the drain. I felt depressed.

I began to question whether the progress I had made was real. I wondered if there was truly any hope for me. I punched out the ref and had to serve a ninety-day suspension. For that, Coach demanded I go see Dr. Colón.

She gave it to me straight: "Paco," she began, "I want you to become the best person—and boxer—you can be. But to do that, you need to tame the beast," she said. "We need to kick things up a notch."

We talked again about the need for me to control my anger. More so, I needed to control my reaction to whatever ticked me off. This time, Dr. Colòn asked me to try a more simple technique. It was supposed to allow me to control my rage before I acted on it.

Now, when I sensed I was losing control, I was to close my eyes. Then I was to count to ten. The only problem with this idea was that I couldn't do it in the ring. If I closed my eyes there for ten seconds, I'd get flattened. I told Dr. Colòn that, and she said she would speak to El Buho. She'd see if there were any boxing techniques I could use to keep my cool. I rolled my eyes at the thought.

It was the following Friday night when El Buho told me his story.

He was closing up the gym. All the boxers were on their way out. Before I left, he asked me to stick around. "Paco," he began. "I spoke to Dr. Colòn today. We've come up with some ideas to help you in the ring."

"Great," I said.

"But first, there's something I want to tell you."

"Okay." I noticed the seriousness in his voice.

He walked out of his office and stood next to the ring. I followed close behind him. He ran his hands up and down the ropes. "Did you know I wasn't a gifted athlete growing up?" he said. I shook my head. The truth was that I had never even imagined Coach Castillo as a kid. He continued, "I didn't have a love for boxing either. I found my way into the ring pretty much the same way you did."

"Through a psychologist's office?" I asked.

"No," Coach Castillo said. "My father. He said using my fists to box was better than using them on the playground, or in the classroom."

"You got into fights at school?"

"Si. All the time," said Coach Castillo. "At school, after school, on the weekends. I was constantly getting in trouble. I was headed for bad things, Paco, perhaps a life behind bars. I got mixed up with a bad crowd, like your brother did. Luckily, my dad had a friend who was a prison guard. He took me on a tour like the one I set up for you. I saw where I'd end up if I didn't change my ways." He squeezed my arm. "I was a lot like you, chico."

It was all making sense. That's why he was so focused on getting me into the gym. I reminded him of himself. And that's why he wasn't giving up on me, either. "How old were you when you started boxing?" I asked.

"I was older than you, about fourteen," he said. "And I didn't know what to make of it at first. I certainly didn't know how to box. But I worked hard, like you. And I made it, all the way to the PAL championship and the Olympic trials. Then I decided to become a coach. I knew I had gone as far as I could in the sport. Boxing has given me everything, especially my sense of value," El Buho added. "But more than anything, it helped me to control my version of el fuego."

I smiled. Never did I expect Coach Castillo to open up to me so much. Nor did I think anyone had the same problem as I did. To find out that it was my trainer was inspirational. The man I was looking at had total control over his emotions. This gave me the hope that some day I would as well.

"I would feel my rage start to take over in the ring. I'd begin to sense I was losing it," Coach Castillo said. "It was in those moments, when I focused all of my energy on dancing. That's what I was talking to Dr. Colòn about. That's what made me realize it was time to tell you about me."

"Dancing?" I asked.

"Si, bailando," El Buho explained. "I focused on my footwork until I was able to get back to my game plan. Our goal, Paco," he added, "is to never have another incident like the Godwin fight. Never. To do that, you need to become a dancer—like me." He leaned in close to me. "Paco, you have so much natural talent. I think you can become a champion."

"A champion. Me?" I spoke these words aloud and nearly cried. I never thought much of myself. But just knowing someone thought I could be champ was almost too much to take. "Thank you." I whispered.

El Buho laughed. "Before we make you the champ, chico, we have to make you a dancer."

I wondered how I would become a dancer. After all, I could barely keep a beat. Then again, I didn't have much of a choice. One more disqualification and I would have to sit out a year. I was beginning to like boxing too much to miss twelve months. Besides, if I wanted to become champion, I needed to get back in the ring.

The following night, back in the gym, I forced myself to dance. It was hard, because all I wanted to do was fight. Footwork did not come as easily to me as punching did. Yet, as Coach Castillo reminded me, it was basic to a boxer's success.

According to El Buho, I needed to be light on my feet. It would allow me to attack and defend at any time. I was great at attacking. My natural instincts allowed me to throw quick and powerful combinations. But if I weren't light on my feet, bigger opponents would knock me out.

I understood that. But I didn't like the idea of going backward. It wasn't in my makeup to retreat. "I haven't seen many boxers your age with your heart. You never back up, that's true. But it's dangerous," Coach Castillo said. "Unless you know exactly what you intend to do, it will backfire on you. Moving your feet will determine how well you can use your heart to your advantage. And how quickly you'll be able to control el fuego."

So I learned to dance. I practiced keeping my weight balanced and staying on the balls of my feet. This way, I could quickly spin or retreat to safety, whatever might be necessary. After a while, my sparring partners seemed to move in slow motion.

"Imagine what you look like to them," El Buho said, chuckling. "You're gonna be a ghost out there. They won't be able to touch you."

Coach Castillo would often take on the role of my opponent. We'd square off against each other for hours every day. He'd have me shift and shuffle my feet quickly. He said that would prevent me from being caught flat-footed.

We tweaked everything during those three months following the Godwin fight. El Buho had me switch stances, changing which foot I put in front. And he had me work my calf muscles, mostly by jumping rope and riding the stationary bike.

"Your movement, your punches and your strategy all have to be in sync," he said. "So, you need to constantly be thinking about your footwork. These thoughts will distract you from feeling angry or out of control."

I have to say, it seemed to be working.

CHAPTER TWELVE

TAMING THE BEAST

I dropped my next fight, but that was okay. At least I didn't let el fuego dictate the outcome. And El Buho said I improved, too. Still, I hated being 0-2. I wanted to win one badly.

Next up for me was a fellow Puerto Rican, Virgilio Ortiz, from Trenton, New Jersey. Although he had yet to lose, this was only Ortiz's second amateur fight. So I came in as the more seasoned boxer—by one bout.

The word on Ortiz was that he liked to sit back and let the action come to him. The odds seemed to be in my favor. Ortiz was one of those boxers who regularly took two punches to throw one. I was happy to hear that my job was to take the fight to him.

According to El Buho, Ortiz was the perfect candidate to jump on in a hurry. Coach Castillo's game plan was for me to come out jabbing. I'd set Ortiz up for a big hook to the head, his reported weakness.

El Buho warned me, though, not to get lured into a trap. Ortiz's strategy could be to let me come in nice and close. And once there, he'd hit me with everything he had. El Buho said he had seen it before. Some boxers were skilled at letting their opponents think they were winning. They would then strike back when their opponent least expected it.

"I've seen boxers come out thinking the fight was theirs," said Coach Castillo. "They'd press the action. Then, the other guy would seem to steal a round or two. So be relentless in pouring on the pressure, Paco," he told me. "Only, don't get cocky. And don't get caught. Move in and out without getting tagged.

It's time to punch your dance card, chico."

The fight was held inside the local National Guard Armory. When the bell rang, I did what I had been instructed. I moved in to establish my left jab from the get-go. I bounced on the balls of my feet, sticking my jab in Ortiz's face. I then danced away.

Occasionally, I'd throw a hook at Ortiz's head. I wanted to see if he was ready for it. In each instance, he was. So I kept banging away, trying to score points. It was clear that at the end of the first round, I was in the lead. I had been on the offensive for the entire two minutes. I was the only one in the ring really doing anything.

That all changed in Round Two. Ortiz seemed to come alive. When I backed him into the ropes, he shot back with two picture-perfect punches. One was a straight right hand. The other was a straight left. They found my head. Not only did they score points, but they stung a little, too.

He had gotten me before I could get away. When I did put some distance between us, I staggered rather than danced. Now I was worried. El Buho had told me to be aware of this, and now it was happening. Every time I got in close to pop him, Ortiz would block my punch. Then he'd send me on my way. And his head shots were starting to hurt.

It was a little more than midway through the second round when el fuego arrived. As a result, I started to lose control. I stopped dancing and started flailing away. I left myself wide open. Just as the round was coming to a close, Ortiz tagged me with an uppercut. It knocked me into the ropes.

In my corner, El Buho had to sit me down on the stool. My body was in the ring, but my mind was not. I was in that place where my killer instinct fueled el fuego. El Buho was talking, but I didn't hear him. "Paco!" he shouted, slapping his hands on my headgear. "Paco!"

I snapped out of it. My eyes opened wider, and my vision got a bit sharper. Staring into my trainer's eyes, I saw a look of desperation come over his face. "Last round, chico, and you're blowing it," he said.

"You're getting suckered, just like I warned you about. You're losing your cool."

I breathed deeply, trying to clear my head of the cobwebs. It wasn't working. "What do I do?" I asked him.

"You move in for the kill," El Buho said. "You feel that anger inside of you?"

"Si," I answered, staring at Ortiz.

"Okay. Hide that anger in your feet. Don't let him know it's there, or what's coming. Dance around this guy until he is seeing two of you. Then, take that anger from your feet and explode!"

I must have had a strange expression on my face, because Coach Castillo almost laughed. "That's right, Paco. You move in and you stay in," he explained. "You know now that he's going to fire back. Be ready for it, dance, and then explode. It's time. You're ready to use el fuego as your strength. Just control it!"

Ding!

"Control, then explode!"

I went out for Round Three intent on beating Ortiz at his own game. I was more fired up and excited then I ever remembered being. It was like something had clicked. I finally understood that el fuego was both my greatest weakness and my greatest strength. Now I just had to control it. Bringing out el fuego too early would cost me the fight.

The final two minutes of the bout began as the

first did. Ortiz sat back waiting for me to walk into a left-right combination. Control it, I thought to myself, as I danced. Control it.

Finally, I felt Ortiz getting frustrated. He was throwing wild punches that weren't landing. I pushed forward. Only this time, I knew what he'd do. And I was ready for it.

Ortiz blocked my jab and snapped off a straight right. It was exactly what I thought he'd throw. I deflected it with my left hand and danced to my left. This opened up a clear path for me to hit him on the chin. I quickly summoned el fuego out of my feet and into my right fist. Then I exploded, catching Ortiz with a hard right to his face. It was an impressive punch. Ortiz grunted as my glove slammed into his forehead. He looked dazed.

I knew enough not to get caught admiring my work. I was careful not to stick around. I danced away into the center of the ring. I had the upper hand once again. I now had Ortiz chasing after me. Time was running out for him, and he knew it. He came in hard and fast. That was his big mistake. I was ready to do what I had wanted to do all night.

First, I backed him up with a jab to the head. Then, I threw a sharp hook to the body. He dropped his hands so as to block my next body shot. But I crossed him up. I went upstairs, and snapped his head back with a left hook, then a right. After that, I went back to the body. I heard El Buho yelling at me to keep moving. So I danced away and inspected the damage.

Ortiz wasn't out on his feet. But his eyes told me he knew he no longer had a chance. He was a warrior, though. He came in yet again. I threw a crisp left hook that nailed him square on the temple. I knew it was going to be the last punch of the night. So did the ref. As Ortiz hit the canvas, he signaled the end to the fight. I had won my first bout—with a knockout!

I realized I never would have won had it not been for Coach Castillo. Without my ability to dance, I would have lost for sure.

We headed for the locker room. El Buho asked me how I felt now that I had my first victory. "I was just thinking how much I like boxing," I said, "despite all the rules."

Coach Castillo laughed. "Yeah, winning helps you feel the love."

"No, it's more than that," I said. "I love the feeling I get when I know I'm doing everything right. When I'm in control of el fuego. I've never felt that before tonight."

"That's a special feeling," said El Buho.

"I know," I said. "Once I did what I was supposed to do, my body and mind were like one. There was no way I was going to lose."

El Buho smiled.

"I've been watching Henry's tapes," I continued. "You know, the ones of Olympic boxing matches."

"Yeah?" answered Coach Castillo.

"I think I want to win the Olympic gold some day."

El Buho put his hand on my shoulder. "And I want to help you do it," he said. "You know, Paco," he added. "In many ways, you're the boxer I was born to coach."

Several months later, I sat at a picnic table across from JoJo. We were in the prison courtyard, reading an article about me in the paper. Since my fight with Ortiz, my record had gone from 1-2 to 12-2. I was making quite a name for myself. When JoJo finished reading, he put the paper down and smiled. "Man, it sounds like you're on your way to the world championship, Paco." He punched me lightly in the arm, jokingly. "You still gotta watch my left, though, little brother."

I smiled. It was the first time I didn't have to meet JoJo behind glass. We were actually allowed to be in each other's company. It was April, so we sat outside. The courtyard was where prisoners with good behavior could meet with visitors.

"You're really sticking with boxing, huh?" he asked.

"Si," I responded. "It's one of the best things in my life right now."

JoJo nodded. "What's another?"

"Coming here to see you," I said.

I caught him grinning. "Well, hopefully you won't have to do it much longer."

"What do you mean?" I asked.

"I just found out there's a chance I might get out of here soon," he said.

"Really? How soon?" I was starting to get excited.

"I'm eligible for parole in three years," he said.

"Three years? That's good, right?" Although I tried to sound excited, three years seemed like a long time.

"Well, that's a lot better than what they originally told me."

"That's great, JoJo," I said.

"Then I can come see you fight," he said. He took another playful swing at my arm.

We sat quietly for the next few minutes. Then, JoJo's voice became more serious. "Paco, do you think Dad will come visit me before I get out of here?"

"I don't know," I said. "You know how Dad can be. It might take some time."

JoJo stared into the distance. "That's exactly what I've got—plenty of time."

CHAPTER THIRTEEN

PUTTING OUT THE FIRE

Over the next three years, I worked hard. When my killer instinct reared its head in the ring, I danced. At home and at school, I counted to ten. My reward was that I just about wiped my record clean.

In the meantime, I added to my ring record. After my terrible start, I won thirty-two straight bouts. My new-found footwork kept me out of harm's way. Yet the fire inside me still burned. Now, though, I was in control of it.

I was a sixteen-year-old sophomore in high school. I had put on twenty pounds in three years, most of it muscle. I was developing into a genuine athlete. My body no longer hid my strength. It showed it off.

I had also become a gym rat. I was at my happiest when I was either training or boxing. I loved the gym. It was a magical place, one that made me feel special. Every chance I got, I watched the other boxers. I would take mental notes on things that worked. Then, I would apply them the next time I climbed through the ropes.

I would also stick around to talk with the older boxers and trainers. I'd often arrive early to do my homework at ringside. I'd watch sparring sessions in between solving algebra problems and writing essays.

My folks were happy, too. They knew where I was every day and night. And I was keeping out of trouble and getting good grades. I even made the honor roll at Rock River High. For that, my dad told me he threw out the military school brochure.

The extra pounds meant I was moving up in weight class. My next fight would have me up against a 135-pound eighteen-year-old. He was an undefeated slugger from Philadelphia named Anthony Watts.

"Just climbing into the ring shows courage, Paco," said Coach Castillo. He was busy taping my hands before my bout with Watts. "But courage is fairly common among boxers. You want to be uncommon. In boxing, you have to train your body and your mind to accept pain. I think we've done that. Now we're ready to take your game to the next level. This will be your toughest fight."

He glanced up to make sure I was paying attention. "Boxing is one of the few sports where the stronger will overcomes the better skill. What you don't have in skills, you make up for in heart," Coach added. "Now, this guy may be bigger than you. But I'm guessing he doesn't have your smarts, your instincts or your heart. Now, go out there and prove me right."

Henry Garcia held up the middle rope for me to climb through. I scanned the crowd inside the legendary Blue Horizon in North Philadelphia. This was my first fight in a real boxing hall. Even more important, this was my first bout in the prestigious Middle Atlantic PAL tournament. El Buho won this same tournament before falling short of his Olympic dream. Part of the reason I wanted to get to the Olympics was for my coach.

It was close to 100 degrees inside the Blue Horizon that night in late March. But I didn't care. I was ready to show everyone that I could beat Anthony Watts. Granted, I was only sixteen and not as seasoned. But I had logged more time in the gym than anyone else at the PAL. I had paid my dues. It was my time.

I danced a bit as I waited for Watts to join me in the ring. I knew he was on his way when I heard the crowd roar. After climbing the steps, he jumped clear over the ropes. He welcomed the standing ovation he received.

"Don't let him psyche you out, Paco," said El Buho. "Fight your fight."

I nodded as Henry slipped my mouthpiece past my teeth and tightened my headgear. I looked up into the balcony, which hung over the ring. It seemed as if you could reach up and touch the fans. I heard a couple of them giving it to me. They let me know that they had come to see Watts flatten me.

I knew I had to block them out—not let them get into my head. I knew I couldn't let my killer instinct get the best of me, and cause me to lose. I could deal with getting hit by a solid punch, but letting my demons win was unacceptable. Still, the crowd booing me was starting to make me angry.

Watts sauntered up to me and sneered. He kept that look on his face while the referee gave us our instructions. He inched closer, so that his face was nearly touching mine. His breath stunk, and he knew it. That's why he breathed heavily right into my nose. He was trying to intimidate me. I started dancing a bit more, turning my focus away from him.

We touched gloves and returned to our respective corners. We stared at each other one last time before the bell rang. It was time to get it on.

Ding!

We both came out cautiously. The report on Watts was that he had a big left hook. But he didn't use it as much as he should. He had a reputation as a headhunter when he should have gone to the body. My plan was to stay at least an arm's length away. Dart in, throw combinations and get out.

I readied myself for a shot to the head while looking for an opening. I didn't have to wait long.

Watts threw his trademark right, straight at my head. I sidestepped the punch. I could feel the wind it generated as it grazed past my ear. I shuffled my feet, planted them, and came back with a right of my own. I caught Watts in the abdomen, a nice power punch. It must have hurt. Watts looked surprised.

I didn't stop there. Forgetting El Buho's advice, I moved closer to engage in a little inside fighting. After missing with a left uppercut, I missed with a right cross. As a result, I was off-balance—and wide open. Watts took advantage. He drilled me with a left-right combination to the nose. The punches knocked me backward.

There was still time left in the first round, and already I was in trouble. I began to lose control. The sight of my own blood did it. Coach Castillo and Henry could sense it. Over the roar of the crowd, I could hear them yelling at me to relax. I dismissed them. I thought I was better than Watts. I knew I could inflict as much pain on him as he could on me. More even.

These thoughts took over. Moving forward again, I threw about six or seven punches that weren't even close. I was punching as hard and as fast as I could. My game plan had gone out the window, and I was getting beaten badly.

I neglected my defense, walking straight into a left jab. The punch snapped my neck back like a bobble head doll. Now, I was truly hurt and unsure of what to do. But I caught a glimpse of Dr. Colòn, sitting next to my father at ringside. It all came back to me. Dance, Paco, I said to myself. Start dancing.

I tried my best to move my feet in a dazzling blur. I had practiced my footwork so much that I was lightning fast. This was the only reason I survived the round. Watts simply couldn't catch me.

"Que haces, Paco? What's going on out there?" Coach Castillo asked me as I sat down on the stool between rounds. "You had me worried."

"Y yo tambien," said Henry, wiping my bloody nose with a towel. "Me too."

"I almost went to that place again," I said.

"But you didn't," said El Buho.

"No, I didn't," I replied.

"Good," he said. "You're learning. And now you've got Watts thinking. He's in for a long night, wouldn't you say?"

"Si," I answered with determination in my voice.

"And now you know if he hits you, you won't go down," said Coach Castillo. "But don't stand there and trade punches with him. Keep making him come after you. Pick your shots. That's how you'll win. Comprende, chico?"

I nodded. I was ready. I stood up for the start of Round Two.

Ding!

I remember not being mad anymore. It didn't matter that Anthony Watts had bloodied my face. I was totally focused on my task. I had cooled el fuego—I had tamed the beast.

Round Two did not begin like the first one. Neither of us was content to circle around each other. It was what's called "go time." After banging at each other a bit, Watts thought he saw an opening. He moved in quickly to exploit it. Only, I was waiting for him. I blocked his left jab, then responded with a left hook, right-cross combination. I tagged him pretty well with the second shot. But it wasn't enough to hurt him. So I quickly got back on my horse and made him come after me.

I did this same thing five more times over the course of the second round. At the end of four minutes, I had a commanding lead.

Coach Castillo met me in my corner with a huge smile on his face. "Muy bien, Paco. Muy bien," he said. "Great round! You did everything right, from start to finish. That was the best round you've ever fought. Listen to them," he added, glancing up into the balcony. "You hear that?"

I turned my head slightly to listen to the crowd at the Blue Horizon. They had turned on local boy Anthony Watts, and were loudly booing him. A good number of them were cheering me on.

"That's because not only are you winning, but you're uncovering his weaknesses," Coach Castillo said. "You're proving how good a boxer you are. If you really want to hear your name, go out and do it some more."

I did what my trainer asked. I went out and kicked butt. Bobbing, weaving, dodging and dancing, I handed a frustrated Anthony Watts his first-ever defeat. I proved stronger and faster. Because of it, I eliminated Watts from the tournament.

The standing ovation I received said a lot. It meant I had defied the odds and won some hearts in the process. But it felt better to know El Buho was proud. So was my dad, who met me at the bottom of the steps. He told me just how pleased he was, too. I knew it before he even spoke, though. Behind my father was Dr. Colòn, wearing a smile even bigger than El Buho's.

It was the reaction of these folks that made me smile. Yes, I had won a fight I wasn't even supposed to be in. But more important was that I had tamed the beast. I kept my killer instinct in check and did what I needed to do. And, man, did it feel great!

CHAPTER FOURTEEN

EL MATADOR

Paco "El Matador" Diaz. That's what the newspaper reporter called me in his column. El Buho got his nickname much in the same way. A reporter wrote that Felix Castillo resembled an owl peeking out from behind his gloves.

From the Watts fight on, I was known as El Matador, in English "The Killer." It was a strange nickname. You would think The Killer would be a powerful puncher who knocks his opponents out. But that wasn't my style at all. According to the writer, he chose El Matador because I reminded him of a bullfighter. Not because I moved in for the kill, but because I was light on my feet. A matador is known for his quickness, not his killer instinct.

At first, I didn't like the name. It wasn't tough enough. Eventually, though, I grew to love it. It had a bit of truth to it. Yes, I had a killer instinct. But, like a matador, I was able to keep it in check. My nickname fit me well.

In order to live up to my name, I had to become an even better dancer. Even though I now had one tournament win, it was only going to get harder. It was back to work in the gym.

For the next week, I worked on every aspect of my game. El Buho would have me shadowbox. Then he'd have me work the heavy bag, speed bag, and double-end bag. After that came some glove work with Henry. I'd follow the old man around the ring, trying to land punches on his soft catcher's mitts. After a short break, it was some jump rope, and then sparring. By the end of each night, I was wiped.

Throughout, I'd work on my footwork. I'd work on something slightly different every day. For instance, one day, I'd practice squaring off against a southpaw, a left-handed boxer. That meant circling to my left and throwing lead right hands. The next day, I'd work on fighting on the inside with short hooks and uppercuts.

The night before my next fight, Coach Castillo learned who my opponent was. He was from Camden, New Jersey, and had recently been discharged from juvenile detention. He was sixteen, like me, with a record that was already garnering him headlines. It wasn't a ring record, though. Now he was looking to get his name in the paper again. This time, he hoped it would be for knocking me out.

The fight was set to go off at the Blue Horizon at eight o'clock. At seven, Coach Castillo dropped me off in front of the auditorium. Neither my dad nor Dr. Colòn were going to be able to make the fight. My mom never watched me in the ring. She'd go to church instead during my fights and pray I didn't get hurt.

I ran up the stairs and headed for the locker room. I was anxious to get in the ring. I wasn't nervous about facing a boxer who had been in prison. I did think about JoJo, however. I thought about his life behind bars. It made me sad. But as quickly as the thought entered my head, it left. I shifted my focus back to the ring. Any loss of focus during a fight could lead to an injury, not to mention defeat.

Coach Castillo brought me back to earth. He could sense things. His nickname said as much about his wisdom as it did about the way he fought. "Wake up, chico," he said. "I know you just put in a great week in the gym. But, you don't know anything about this guy. Who are you to take anyone lightly?' he added. "This guy could knock you out with one punch."

I remember thinking this wasn't a very inspirational pep talk. But he was right. All I had was a good amateur record and one tournament win. I had no right to be cocky. And I had no business spacing out minutes before a fight.

I had my bearings when I entered the ring to

stare down Antoine Lydell. He was shorter than I was. But he looked stronger. And he was more mean-looking than I could ever pretend to be.

The corner of his mouth was turned up. As he breathed, it sounded as though he was growling. Like a bear. I wasn't scared, mind you. But I'd be lying if I didn't admit to worrying. It wasn't that I was concerned about getting hurt. I was more worried about him forcing me to lose control. I didn't want to have another setback. I was making great progress.

The fight started out like my last one. It was unlike the majority of amateur boxing matches. In most amateur fights, the boxers are well aware of how short a bout is. So they start swinging quickly. By contrast, there's no rush in a professional fight. Boxers in the pros have time to conserve energy and change their fight plan. In the amateurs, you have to get busy in a hurry.

So, when Lydell came out slowly, I noticed his pro style. His way of fighting was the exact opposite of mine. I was an amateur boxer and, in many ways, a classic one. The rules favored my approach. The boxer who threw flurries, scored points, and avoided getting hit stood the best chance at winning. I had done that in my previous fight, and it secured my victory. I won even though I didn't really hurt Watts at all. I was a boxer, not a fighter.

In amateur boxing, the force of a blow doesn't count. A knockdown blow receives no more credit than a regular shot. It's scored as a single punch and doesn't necessarily give that boxer the round.

Such a scenario was tailor made for me and my dancing feet. Not for the crowd at the Blue Horizon, though. Sure, true fight fans appreciated a well-executed plan and good footwork. But the rest of the folks wanted to see a knockout. For them, a knockout was even better than an upset.

That's why the same folks who loved me a week ago hated me tonight. I didn't bring a big punch to the table. Luckily for them, Antoine Lydell did. And the audience held their breath. They were waiting for him to unload his huge right hand on me. As far as I could tell, the crowd expected the little Latino to be knocked out by his stronger opponent. They were clearly in Lydell's corner.

They ended up disappointed. Shortly after the fight began, I stuck my left jab in Lydell's face. I kept it there all night. I set him up time and again for a quick right hand to the head. Then I would boogie away.

At the end of the first round, I had Lydell backed into the corner. I let loose with a barrage of jabs and hooks. But as I connected, I thought ahead. I didn't want to overstay my welcome. So I hurried back out onto the dance floor. Even the chorus of boos didn't bother me. I was in control, in more ways than one. It was beautiful.

By the middle of the second round, he had

stopped growling. His grimace was gone. He looked frustrated.

When the final bell sounded and the ref lifted my hand, I was thrilled. The crowd stopped booing to applaud. I was El Matador, a boxer, and a good one at that.

"So, you're gonna win the championship of the Police Athletic League," said JoJo. "Ain't that something."

"I have to win a bunch more times to get to the title fight. I've got a long way yet. Besides, it's just a local tournament."

"Still, you're doing awesome."

"Thanks," I said. "Too bad you can't be at ringside."

JoJo laughed. "I don't think the warden will let me take a field trip." I started laughing, too. "But I'm getting closer to my parole hearing."

"How close?" I asked.

He smiled. "Close enough, Paco." JoJo refused to tell me when his parole hearing was. He wanted to protect me from getting my hopes up, in case he didn't get out. "Anyway," he continued, "when I do get out of here, maybe you could teach me how to box."

"I'd love to. But it's not all about big muscles, JoJo." I smiled. "I mean, if you were to land a punch against a guy like me, you might knock me out. But, to be honest, I don't think you'd be able to touch me."

JoJo laughed again. "I like that attitude. You bring that into the ring and you will win that championship."

"It's not going to be easy," I said. "I'm still learning how to box, you know?"

"Listen to me, hermano. And this is coming from someone who knows," JoJo said. "Never doubt what you can do. I doubted myself and let other people tell me what they thought I should do. I forgot everything I knew, everything I had been taught."

I didn't know how to respond. So I didn't say anything.

"You know what?" said JoJo. "You're my brother, so I'm biased. But I'm proud of you, Paco. From what you've told me, someone with a killer instinct could never become a boxer. You've got heart, little brother."

"You've got heart, too," I said in return.

CHAPTER FIFTEEN

WHO'S NEXT?

Standing in the ring at the Blue Horizon, I blocked out the noise. I focused on my opponent as the referee went over his instructions.

It was the championship match in the lightweight division of the Middle Atlantic PAL tournament. I had my game face on.

Across from me stood Sergio Campos, a tough Mexican-American from Atlantic City. He had only one loss to his name. He was a hard puncher with fast hands and an even faster mind. He had a history of making his opponents look foolish. I didn't intend for that to happen. I could handle defeat. But if I was going to lose, I would do so with style. My goal, however, was to win.

I had won three more times in the tournament to get to this point. And I was getting better each time

I stepped into the ring. My record, at 37-2, wasn't all that far behind Campos's 42-1. This was the match all the experts were saying would be the best of the tournament.

My fan section at ringside was at full strength for this fight. Sitting next to Dr. Colòn and my dad were Ramon and Juan, my buddies from school. My mom and baby sister Marisol had come for the first time, too. Even Principal Grace was there to see me take the title.

About a minute before the bout, I looked back at them one more time. That was when I saw my brother. Making his way down the aisle was JoJo. I watched as he approached my mother, giving her a big hug. Then, he lifted my sister high into the air and kissed her on the cheek. Finally, he made his way over to my father. They stared at each other for a moment, before Dad pulled JoJo toward him. I stood there watching them hug each other. I was near tears.

Coach Castillo looked over at my family and smiled down at me. He then slapped my headgear. "Focus, chico. They'll be waiting for you after the fight."

I took a final glance toward the stands. JoJo was cheering louder than anyone. Our eyes met, and he smiled. I never felt as happy in my life as I stared at him. He was standing next to my parents with Marisol on his shoulders. He had kept his release date a secret, hoping to surprise me. Boy, did he ever!

I felt a surge of strength coursing through my veins. I looked up at El Buho. He gave me a nod of assurance—and one final piece of advice. "Remember, Paco," he said. "The boxer with heart is the one who never looks for a way out. You've learned to live with your problem. You didn't look for an easy way out. You've fought hard to keep it in check," he added. "I respect you for that. A lot of us here tonight already know you're a winner." He looked into the stands. "But I want you to show us all what kind of boxer you are. Give us your best tonight, chico."

Ding!

Ten minutes later, I was standing in the middle of the ring. The ref was holding my left wrist with his right hand. He held Sergio Campos' right wrist with his other hand. The three of us stood waiting for the ring announcer to reveal the decision. "We have a unanimous decision," the announcer said slowly.

I looked over at El Buho. He winked.

"The winner, and new Middle Atlantic PAL light weight champion ... Paco El Matador Diaz!" The crowd went crazy as the ref raised my hand up in the air.

First I gave Campos a hug. I told him in his ear how he had fought a great match. Then I threw my arms around El Buho. I noticed he had a few tears running down his face. Over his shoulder, I saw my dad applauding and my mom crying. I saw Dr. Colòn and Marisol jumping up and down. But I was looking for JoJo. I found him, in the aisle, trying to get through the crowd. He stopped next to the ring. With his right hand over his heart, he pointed to me with his left. "You're the best, little brother."

I gave him the same salute in return. I felt so happy that he was a part of our family again.

Just then, the media muscled its way through the ropes and into the center of the ring. As the flashbulbs went off, a flood of questions came my way.

"Hey, Matador, will you be back next year to defend your title?"

"What about the national PAL Championships next month? Do you plan to participate?"

"Then there's the Pennsylvania Golden Gloves?"

"How about the U.S. Championships?"

"The Olympics?"

"El Matador, do you hope to represent your country in the ring?"

El Buho jumped in and responded on my behalf. "We're going to enjoy this victory. El Matador is going to spend some time with his family. Then, knowing this kid, he'll be back in the gym. We'll take a long hard look at how we can continue to get better. That's our objective, to improve," he said. "Of course, our ultimate goal is to represent the United States in the Olympic Games." Then, turning to me, he said. "Do you want to add anything, Paco?"

I smiled up at him. I looked out at the sea of

reporters in front of me and spoke from my heart. "This is only the beginning," I said. "Because, as you may have noticed, I've got this fire inside."

TEST YOURSELF...ARE YOU A PROFESSIONAL READER?

Chapter 1: El Fuego

What is shadowboxing?

Why do boxers put Vaseline on their faces before and during a fight?

Does a boxer need to control his/her emotions during a fight? Explain.

ESSAY

Paco talks about a time when anger used to control his life. Write about a moment when your anger got the best of you. What did you learn from this experience?

Chapter 2: Recess and
Chapter 3: A Bad Seed

Paco is bilingual. What does bilingual mean? How did he become bilingual?

Who is Butchie LaManna?

Why did Paco's parents send him to St. Joe's?

ESSAY

In Chapter 3, Paco explains that he admires his brother, JoJo. Who is someone in your life that you admire? Explain why you look up to this person.

Chapter 4: Killer Instinct

Who is Dr. Adriana Colon?

What do the Spanish words "El Fuego" mean?

What does Dr. Colon think that Paco should purchase to calm his anger problem?

ESSAY

This chapter displays how much Paco has disappointed his parents with his actions. Describe a situation in your life when you disappointed someone that cared about you. How did this situation make you feel?

Chapter 5: El Buho

What was the deal Mr. Felix Castillo and Paco made when Paco came into the gym looking for a punching bag?

Why did Paco continue to pound the punching bag after he struck it the first time?

Why did Paco finally decide to take boxing lessons from El Buho?

ESSAY

As Paco unleashes his fury on the punching bag, his natural athletic talent is shown in his actions. Write about a time when you discovered a hidden talent of your own.

Chapter 6: Fire Down Below

What character traits did Paco's dad think his son would learn from boxing?

Why was Paco nervous about adjusting to the rules of boxing?

Where did El Buho tell Paco he'd eventually end up if he didn't find a way to control his rage?

ESSAY

In Chapter 6, Paco furthers his reputation as a quitter. Give an example of an activity that you quit. Why do you think it is so important to finish things you begin?

Chapter 7: Therapy

When El Buho took Paco away from the gym, where did they go?

What did the prisoners call the block of prison cells that lined the main hallway?

Who did Paco see as he was leaving prison? What difference did he notice in this person's appearance?

ESSAY

In this chapter, we are taken behind the scenes of a prison. What did you learn about prison in Chapter 7? What scared you the most about prison? Why is prison a place to stay far, far away from?

Chapter 8: The Visit

Why did JoJo rip up all of the letters that he wrote to Paco?

Why did JoJo encourage Paco to continue boxing?

What scene in this chapter shows that Paco has begun to tame "El Fuego?"

ESSAY

JoJo speaks to Paco in this chapter about the importance of playing sports and getting involved in activities. Why do you think that playing sports or finding other constructive hobbies is so important? What sports or hobbies do you enjoy?

Chapter 9: Ground Rules and
Chapter 10: Out of Control

What two rules did El Buho give Paco for his day off from boxing?

What did Paco learn in "Boxing 101?"

How did Paco react to adversity during his bout with David Godwin?

ESSAY

In Chapters 9 and 10, El Buho continues to show that he is interested in helping Paco become a better boxer, and a better person. Detail a time in your life when you assisted someone. How did this act of giving of yourself make you feel? Why is it important to help other people?

Chapter 11: Dancing and
Chapter 12: Taming the Beast

How did Paco feel about his actions as he reflected upon his fight with David Godwin?

Why did El Buho think that Paco needed to learn to dance in the ring?

Who did Paco defeat for his first victory?

ESSAY

In these chapters, we get to glance into El Buho's childhood. Like Paco, he learned to tame "El Fuego" with the help of his family. How does your family help you every day? What are a few things that are unique about your family?

Chapter 13: Putting Out the Fire

Why is this chapter entitled "Putting Out the Fire?"

Why did Paco watch the other boxers train when he was in the gym?

Who is Anthony Watts? How many losses did he have before he fought Paco?

ESSAY

Earlier in the book, Paco disappoints his parents. By Chapter 13, Paco's actions have begun to impress his mom and dad. Write about a time in your life when you made your parents, or another family member, proud of you.

Chapter 14: El Matador and
Chapter 15: Who's Next?

How did El Buho get his nickname?

Why was the crowd cheering for Antoine Lydell during his bout with Paco?

Why didn't JoJo tell Paco when he was scheduled to be released from prison?

ESSAY

Congratulations! You have completed another Scobre Press book! After joining Paco on his journey, detail what you learned from his life and experiences. How are you going to use Paco's story to help you achieve your dreams? What did Paco teach you about the importance of controlling your anger?